Willy Waggledagger

A BELT AROUND MY BUM

Little Hare Books
8/21 Mary Street, Surry Hills
NSW 2010 AUSTRALIA

www.littleharebooks.com

Text copyright © Martin Chatterton 2009
Illustrations copyright © Gregory Rogers 2009

First published in 2009

National Library of Australia
Cataloguing-in-Publication entry

Chatterton, Martin.

A belt around my bum / Martin Chatterton ;
illustrator, Gregory Rogers.

978 1 921272 98 1 (pbk.)

Chatterton, Martin. Willy Waggledagger.

For primary school age.

Rogers, Gregory, 1957-

A823.4

Cover design by Luke and Vida Kelly
Set in 12.5/21 pt Stone Informal by Clinton Ellicott
Printed by Griffin Press
Printed in Salisbury, South Australia in September 2009

5 4 3 2 1

Contents

ThorNy HEdgEhogs, achiNg Bums

Eric the ox was going as fast as he could.

Eric didn't believe in doing things quickly. Especially not pulling heavy carts filled with actors, singers, musical instruments, props, costumes and everything else that made up the Black Skulls, the most exciting theatrical performers in England.

Eric's cart was heading south towards Richmond Palace where the Skulls were due to perform for Her Most Glorious and Majestic Queen Elizabeth. Eleven-year-old William Shakespeare, known as Willy Waggledagger to his friends, was the driver. He had been a member of the Skulls for little over a week and was looking forward to this performance more than anything he'd ever looked forward to before. But, right now, all he could think about was his aching bum.

Willy shifted his buttocks on the wooden seat and glanced glumly at a snail creeping along the verge. The snail had been keeping pace with Willy's cart for the past five minutes.

'I could walk faster than this!' grumbled Willy. He glared at Eric's rather smelly behind and twitched the reins. Eric continued to plod slowly up the hill at exactly the same speed he'd been plodding along at since leaving Stratford a week ago.

Yorick, sitting alongside Willy, lifted his shaggy head and gave Willy a sour glance. 'Not pullin' this cart you couldn't, Waggledagger,' he said, before speaking softly to the ox. 'Don't listen to the young pup, Eric, me old mucker. 'E don't know wot 'e's talkin' about.'

Willy turned his attention back to the race between Eric and the snail. He was worried by Yorick's behaviour. The normally chirpy Black Skulls technical wizard, backstage craftsman and all round Mr Fix-It, had been acting most peculiarly for the past few days. And the closer they got to Richmond Forest, the odder he became. He'd even gone off his food! The big man had eaten only half a side of beef for lunch, and left almost a mugful of his barrel of ale untouched.

Not that he was in any danger of fading away. Yorick, perched on the driving board, resembled a mid-sized hairy mountain.

And yet, there was no doubt about it: summink, as the hairy mountain would have said, was up.

Willy kept quiet. Pulling barnacles off the hull of the *Mary Rose* with his eyelids would be easier than getting information out of Yorick when he was in this mood.

In the second cart, Olly Thesp, England's best singer, finest actor and champion pain in the posterior, piped up for the twenty-seventh time that morning. 'Are we there yet?'

Yorick growled softly. He turned and gave Olly one of his special glares.

'Only asking,' muttered Olly. He flopped back sulkily against a bale of canvas and continued oiling his gleaming black beard.

Charlie Ginnell, the Black Skulls manager, was driving the second cart. He raised his eyebrows at Olly's moaning, and winked at Elbows McNamara, who sat beside him.

Elbows was the Skulls Irish fiddler and wizard prop-maker. He winked back at Charlie. 'He does have a point, boss,' he muttered. 'It's been a long week on the road. It's no wonder that people is getting twitchy.'

Some way back, a lonely figure trudged behind the carts, balancing a ventriloquist's dummy on one hand and scooping ox poop into a sack with the other. Minty Macvelli, and his ever-present performing doll, Minimac, had been on poop duty all the way from Vile Towers in Stratford. It was punishment for almost getting Olly killed by the horrible Sir Victor Vile, Commander of the Codpieces, a terrifying protection squad who guarded Queen Elizabeth around the clock.

Willy gave the reins a twitch. 'Come on, Eric!' he yelled. 'Let's see how fast this baby can go!'

For once, Eric responded. He pulled away from the snail and, in a matter of minutes, the cart lurched over the crest of the hill.

Willy gasped.

Spread out below them like a green velvet cape was Richmond Forest. To one side was the palace, its towers gleaming majestically in the last rays of the sun. To the south, the Thames chugged slowly on its way to smelly old London—the City That Never Slops.

Willy gave Yorick a dig in the ribs with his elbow and pointed at the glittering palace lying ahead.

Yorick made a noise that could have been a sigh, or possibly a grunt. Willy bit his lip. This grumpy version of Yorick was beginning to remind Willy of his father.

Willy shivered at a sudden memory of his red-faced, big-mouthed father, sounding off about all the things in the world of which he disapproved. Which was just about everything. But of the many things John Shakespeare hated, the theatre was top of the list. And after the first time Willy ran off with the Black Skulls, he hated it even more.

'Only a lunatic would turn his back on an honest career like tanning, and run off with a bunch of prancing wastrels!' he bellowed at dinner on the night he dragged Willy home. Specks of meat shot from his mouth and sprayed across the table. 'If you so much as *think* about trying anything like that again, I'll give you the hiding of your life!'

Just thinking about that night was enough to make Willy shudder and glance fearfully over his shoulder. Even though he was hundreds of miles from Stratford, the memory of his father made Willy's blood run cold.

Willy sighed and thrust the unpleasant thoughts from his head. Nothing, not even a bad-tempered Yorick, was going to make Willy go back to Stratford ever again.

He cracked the reins once more and Eric, sensing that a well-earned gobful of grass was not too far away, lurched down the hill with more energy than he'd mustered all week.

2

Will Met by Moonlight

The carts rolled into a tunnel formed by the treetops meeting above the track. The green light thickened, low mist swirled around the cartwheels, and an owl hooted from a nearby branch.

Olly stopped oiling his beard and looked around. 'I don't like it,' he whined and hid under a rug.

Willy pulled his tunic closer around him. 'Is it just me,' he asked, 'or is it getting chillier?'

Minty scurried up to Willy's cart. 'I heard tell that this place is haunted,' he said as he clambered aboard and placed Minimac on his knee. Poop duty or no poop duty, Minty wasn't going to be caught on foot in a strange forest. He changed his voice into that of a cackling witch. 'Some say Richmond Forest is the home of the Faerie King.'

There was a muffled squeak from Olly.

'Knock it off, Minty,' said Charlie from the driving board of the second cart. 'You're scaring the actors. And they're easily spooked.'

'Wot a load of old nonsense!' growled Yorick. 'Anyone callin' themselves the Faerie King is a couple of pennies short of a groat, if you arsks me.'

'Which no one did,' said Minty. He leaned between Willy and Yorick and lowered his voice. 'The Faerie King has some mighty powerful magic, Yorick. I'd watch what I said in his kingdom, if I were you. *And* I'll bet this place is stuffed with wood sprites, hobgoblins, elves, trolls, daemons, unicorns, dragons, and leprechauns, too. You name it, it'll be here.'

Yorick snorted and inspected a woodlouse he'd found inside his right ear. 'C'mon, Waggledagger,' he growled. 'Let's get this load of plonkers set up.'

They rolled deeper into the woods.

'You know, this place *is* kind of spooky, Yorick,' whispered Willy. 'And how come you keep peeking into the trees?'

'There's a clearin' five minutes from 'ere,' grunted Yorick, ignoring Willy's question. 'We'll camp there.'

The clearing was large and grassy and hemmed in by closely packed trees. On the far side of the clearing, the track continued on towards the palace.

The Skulls began to set up camp. After a lifetime on the road, when it came to making themselves comfortable, they were slick as a weasel in a butter churn. In no time at all, the carts were parked in a circle, with a cooking fire at the centre, and a kitchen bench set up across the tailboard of the lead cart.

Yorick and Willy began to whip up the evening meal. By the time the cooking pot was bubbling, night had fallen, and the Skulls were hovering hungrily around the fire.

'Stew?' whined Minty, casting an eye over the pot. 'Again? What sort of stew is it this time?'

'Squirrel,' said Yorick, pointing a sharp knife at Minty. 'You don't like it, you can always try yer luck in the forest. You never know, you might catch one o' them blinkin' faeries you've been rabbitin' on about.'

'You can laugh all you like,' said Minty, 'but these woods are no place for an honest man.'

'Well, that's you safe, then, innit?' growled Yorick. 'Now 'op it!'

Minty hopped.

*

A couple of hours later, as Willy cleared away the remains of the meal, he felt about as tired as he'd ever felt. The rest of the Skulls had already clambered into whatever kind of bed they had rigged up for themselves. Only Walden Kemp, the Black Skulls writer and director, was awake. He sat on a log, chewing the end of a clay pipe and scratching notes with a feather quill by the light of the fire. Every so often he'd ball up a sheet of parchment and hurl it into the flames.

'The new play?' said Willy.

'Yes, the new play!' barked Walden. 'Curse it for a fool's errand!'

'Um, any songs in it?' said Willy, doing his best to be helpful.

'Of course there'll be songs, you blithering buffoon! What's the point of having someone like Olly around if you don't give him something to sing? It's the rest of it that's the problem!'

As far as Willy could gather from seeing the Skulls rehearsing during the journey, Walden's new play was a frothy little comedy about a group of idiotic foreign noblemen lost in a forest.

'Maybe put some fart jokes in,' suggested Willy. 'Everyone loves a fart joke. Or bum jokes. Maybe one of the characters could have a funny name?'

'Such as?' snapped Walden. 'Bumface, or Wideload, or Bottom, I suppose?'

Willy nodded. 'Bottom. That's pretty good! And maybe he could have a tail, or some donkey ears or something? That'd get a laugh!'

Walden opened his mouth to speak, then closed it again. He began scribbling furiously. 'You're not as gormless as you look, Waggle-dagger,' he muttered, 'you might just have something there.'

Willy turned back to the dishes. He didn't

want to disturb Walden now he was finally getting some ideas down on parchment. The last thing Willy needed was for the new play to flop. A flop could mean the end of the Black Skulls, and that would mean Willy returning to Stratford—and to his horrible father—with his tail between his legs.

That wasn't going to happen, not if Willy had anything to do with it. He wiped the last bowl clean, rammed some soft cotton rags into his ears to block out the sound of Yorick's snores, and made himself a bed from some costumes in the back of Eric's cart. He lay down and settled miserably into what he was sure would be a restless night.

Three seconds later he was fast asleep.

3

a Bear in the Bush

Willy was floating along a purple river on the belly of a giant pink otter when an eagle made from old shoes pecked him on the nose.

Hard.

'*Ow!*' said Willy and opened his eyes.

Elbows was leaning over him, his finger poised for another nose-flick. The rest of the Skulls, with the exception of Yorick, were huddled behind him.

'It's about time you woke up,' whispered Elbows. 'There's something funny going on.'

'Funny ha-ha or funny peculiar?' said Willy.

Minty and Minimac were cowering behind Elbows's right shoulder. Minty leaned closer. 'Peculiar,' he hissed.

'And scary,' added Minimac.

'A bear!' squeaked Olly, pointing from behind Elbows's other shoulder. 'Look!'

To Willy's surprise, Olly was right. There *was* a bear, quite a big one, lurching from side to side in the shadows at the edge of the clearing.

Olly hauled Willy off the cart and shoved him in the direction of the bear. 'Go on, do something!' he said, and hid behind Charlie, who was hiding behind Minty.

'Me?' said Willy. 'What can *I* do? Why can't Yorick go? He's bigger than me!'

'We can't wake him up,' said Minty. 'Besides, you're quicker on your feet.'

'Might be useful if the bear chases after you,' added Minimac.

'Good idea!' said Charlie. 'Just get the bear

to chase you into the woods for a little bit.'

'What do you mean, "chase me into the woods"? I'll get eaten!'

Walden looked at Willy from where he was crouching behind Elbows's legs and coughed. 'Look, Waggledagger,' he said. 'You have to ask yourself if you *really* want to be a Black Skull, right? Frankly, I'm a bit disappointed in your attitude so far. Look on this as a sort of test.' He smiled encouragingly and nodded in the direction of the bear.

Willy looked at the rest of them. Everyone began inspecting their fingernails or finding interesting specks of lint on their tunics.

Willy sighed. Unless he wanted a quick trip straight back to Stratford and his awful father, it looked like he would have to at least try to do something about the bear.

He grabbed a large frying pan and shuffled across the clearing towards the wild beast.

'That's the ticket, Waggledagger,' said

Charlie as he slid behind the cart. 'That's the fighting, Black Skulls spirit!'

The rest of the Skulls fell silent. All except for Olly, whose teeth were chattering so loudly they almost drowned out Yorick's snores.

Scare the bear, Willy murmured to himself. Nothing to it. Piece of parkin. Just walk up to it and ... and ... and what, exactly?

'Shoo!' he hissed, waving the frying pan. 'Shoo!'

'I don't think that's gonna do much good,' hissed Elbows. 'It's a bloomin' big bear, Waggledagger! Chuck the frying pan at it or something!'

'I *know* it's a bloomin' big bear!' Willy snapped. 'I'm standing closer to it than you are!'

The bear seemed to be getting more and more agitated as Willy moved closer. It swung wildly from side to side.

Willy lifted the frying pan and hurled it

with all his might. The pan wheeled across the clearing. There was an ear-splitting roar. Willy squeaked in terror, turned and ran for his life. The Black Skulls scattered.

'Run!' screamed Minty. 'It's after us!'

Willy ran as fast as he'd ever run before. But suddenly his foot caught on an old tree root and he tumbled onto the ground. Something very large and very angry thudded towards him. It came closer and closer, until a great moon-shadow fell across Willy's back. He knew the end had come.

I'm bear food, he thought.

A second great roar boomed across the camp site. Willy squeezed his eyes shut.

'FLAMIN' FERKINS! WILL YOU GANG OF IDIOTS STOP YER YAMMERIN' AND LET A FELLER GET SOME WELL-EARNED KIP!'

Willy opened one eye. The bad news was that a massive hairy thing was standing over him. The good news was that the massive hairy thing was Yorick. Willy breathed a sigh of relief. Then he saw Yorick's face. The big man was not someone who liked to be woken in the middle of the night.

'I expected more from you, Waggledagger,' said Yorick, fixing Willy with a stare that could have raised a blister on an iceberg.

'But, the b-b-bear,' stammered Willy. He pointed to where the terrible creature stood, still lurching about in the moonlight.

'Give me strenf!' spat Yorick. He stomped across the clearing.

'Yorick!' Willy cried. 'No!'

With the confidence of someone who knew exactly what he was doing, Yorick went straight up to the bear and ripped off a large chunk of its left forepaw.

Willy heard the familiar sound of Olly fainting.

'This yer bear, mates?' said Yorick returning with the chunk of bear. He held up a clump of twigs and leaves and shook it in Willy's face. ''Cos it looks very like a bush from where I'm standin'!'

'It's a bush!' said Willy. 'Just a stupid bush, blowing in the wind!'

'Well, I'll be a baboon's backside,' said Charlie, crawling out from under a pork barrel. 'My flabber is well and truly gasted.'

'I could have sworn that was a bear,' said Elbows, peeking out from beneath a rug in the back of a cart.

'It did *look* like a bear in the dark,' said Walden as he rolled from a hidey-hole he'd found in an old tree stump.

'Bear or no bear, this place is still haunted, I tell you,' said Minty from behind a pile of boxes. 'It was the King of the Faeries playing tricks on us!'

'Get off me, you big cowardly custard!' yelled a muffled voice from underneath Minty. It was Minimac.

Yorick glowered at the Skulls. 'Jist look at you! Like a bunch of panickin' chickens! Pathetic, that's wot it is! Grown men lettin' themselves be spooked by nuffink more than a bush wavin' in the breeze!'

The Skulls hung their heads, traced circles on the ground with their toes and bobbed from side to side. Yorick was right. They were pathetic.

'Now,' said Yorick as he wedged himself back into his bed on the driving board of the cart, 'will you all jist keep the noise down and let a bloke get a bit o' shut-eye before the sun comes up? And fer chuff's sake, get one fing straight! There is no such fing as the King of the flamin' Faeries!' With a final glare around the clearing, Yorick went back to sleep.

There was a short silence, followed by some rustling amongst the trees. Then a figure emerged from the woods.

It was the King of the Faeries.

23

4
a lion amongst laddies

The Skulls knew their visitor was the King of the Faeries because he told them so.

'Good mornin', peasants,' he boomed. 'I am O'Brion, King of the Faeries.'

'Ha!' said Minty. 'In your face, Yorick!'

Yorick sat bolt upright in bed, looked around and spotted the newcomer. Then he put his head in his hands and groaned.

Willy blinked. The King of the Faeries wasn't quite what he would have expected. For a start, he was on the chubby side. He wore a shabby robe, patched with a collection of old rags and bits of tree bark. His dirty black hair hung down in a thick shaggy curtain, decorated here and there with flowers, some of which had almost rotted away. As the King of the Faeries stomped closer to the gaping Skulls, a small mouse poked its nose from his beard and had a look around, before darting back into the undergrowth. The only faerie-like thing about the King was the dainty pair of pink wings that sprouted from his shoulders. But even these were made from bits of cloth and twigs, and had been tied in place with string.

The King of the Faeries walked in a strange tippy-toe fashion. Not that it made a scrap of difference; he still thumped the ground as heavily as ... well, as heavily as Yorick did. Behind him followed a motley collection of animals: a ball of hair that might have been a dog, a one-eyed squirrel with a nasty glint in its eye, a goat, a newt (which was hard to spot at first), three jet-black crows, and a buzzing cloud of flies, mosquitoes and assorted bugs.

All in all, Willy had never seen anyone like him. To be honest, Willy thought the King of the Faeries looked like a bit of a nut. But he was easily as big as Yorick, and he had a strange yellow glint in his eyes, so Willy kept that thought to himself.

The King stopped in front of the Skulls, who were huddled together in the middle of the clearing. Olly looked like he didn't know whether to bow or faint.

'Oi! You there!' said the King, pointing a grimy finger at Yorick. 'How dare you remain seated in the presence of . . . er . . . me? I command you in the name of all fings Faerie to stand and show me due respeck!'

Yorick remained slumped in his bed, not so much as glancing in the King's direction.

Willy thought there was something familiar about the way the King of the Faeries spoke. He sounded just like Yorick.

In fact, now Willy thought about it some

more, the King of the Faeries *looked* a bit like Yorick, too.

Yorick lifted his head and stared wearily at the King of the Faeries. 'I woz worried you'd show up,' he said. 'I kept hopin' you'd 'ave moved somewheres else by now, O'Brion. But 'ere you is, hangin' around like a bad smell. And you don't 'alf 'onk. I can sniff you from 'ere. I s'pose yer still bangin' on about the Queen and all that rubbish about 'er bloomin' belt?'

O'Brion looked offended. 'You know as well as I do that the Golden Girdle belongs to me!'

'Give it a rest, O'Brion, you big galoot!' snapped Yorick. 'That belt belongs to 'er! She can wear it if she wants. Jist face it, you ain't ever gettin' it. She's the *Queen*, fer Gawd's sake!'

The one-eyed squirrel sidled towards Yorick and growled menacingly.

'Easy, Tinkerbell,' said O'Brion. 'The peasant

can't be blamed fer 'is lack of manners. He's a bit uncoof, like.'

'I'm sure Yorick didn't mean anything by his words, Your, erm, Highness,' said Charlie. He was not entirely sure what was going on but he thought he might as well be polite.

'There's no need fer all that bowin' and scrapin' nonsense, Charlie,' said Yorick. 'Not wiv O'Brion. This "Girdle" nonsense is all because the Queen 'ad a belt made from some gold wot woz dug out of this forest. This joker reckons it belongs to 'im jist because the gold came from the forest. It's mad!'

'Yorick,' hissed Charlie. 'This is *royalty* you're talking to!'

'Don't make me laugh!' snapped Yorick.

As Willy watched O'Brion and Yorick argue, a question began to form in his mind.

'Is the King of the Faeries …' stammered Willy. 'He's not your … I mean … is O'Brion your *brother*, Yorick?'

Yorick sighed heavily.

Olly Thesp popped his head out from behind Charlie. 'Your brother is King of the Faeries?' he squeaked.

''Alf-bruvver,' said Yorick, scowling. 'Only me *'alf-bruvver.*'

'You!' scoffed Minty. 'Related to royalty! That'll be the day!'

''E's not royalty! 'E's jist . . . me bruvver!'

'Who 'appens to be King of the Faeries,' said O'Brion loftily.

'Away wiv the bloomin' faeries, more like,' muttered Yorick.

'You never mentioned a brother,' said Charlie.

'Yeah, well,' said Yorick. 'Would you?'

'Bit of a nutter, eh?' said Elbows. 'We've all got them, mate. I remember my old Uncle Ernie . . .' He put a finger to his head and twirled it around.

'SILENCE, LEPRECHAUN!' yelled O'Brion.

He whipped out a long wooden staff from beneath his robes and pointed it at Elbows. 'Nobody makes play of the King of the Faeries! 'Specially not some stinkin' leprechaun.'

'Who are you calling a leprechaun?' cried Elbows.

O'Brion started to shake. Olly slid behind the nearest cart.

'*Mumble gumble shimble blug*, turn this oaf into a slug!' bellowed O'Brion.

Elbows flinched and closed his eyes. He didn't want to be turned into a slug. Even slugs don't want to be slugs.

There was a short pause. Nothing happened.

O'Brion looked at the end of the wooden staff and banged it against the heel of his hand. He pointed it at Elbows again. 'Slug!' he bellowed.

Nothing. O'Brion shook the staff once more, then tucked it back into his robe. 'Technical 'itch,' he snorted in disgust. 'Need to charge up the old magic power. I need that Girdle, see!'

'I thought this belt thing belonged to the Queen?' said Charlie.

'It does,' Yorick said. 'My bruvver jist *finks* it's 'is.' He looked at O'Brion. 'When are you goin' to stop this nonsense and get a real job? One wot fits yer skills. Cesspit cleaner, plague carrier, gravedigger, summink like that?'

O'Brion sat down heavily on the edge of Yorick's cart. 'You've no idea 'ow 'ard it is bein' King of the Faeries, bruv,' he groaned. 'It's bad enough 'aving to look after the forest and all the creatures, not to mention dealin' wiv all them elves and goblins and trolls and wotnot. Don't even get me started on the leprechauns. And on top of it all, that woman has me Girdle. I'll grant you, it ain't wot you might call *technically* mine. But I wants it. And I needs it. And I'm the King, and that's all that matters!'

Willy glanced nervously around the clearing. It was fairly busy, but there was no sign of magical beings—unless you counted the squirrel and the rest of O'Brion's animal friends. Perhaps the elves and whatnot were keeping quiet somewhere out in the forest.

'Anyways,' said Yorick, hoisting himself out of bed and off the cart, 'wot, exackly, do you want wiv us, bruv?'

O'Brion smiled, revealing a blackened row of teeth. 'Oh,' he said, 'I'm checkin' wot side yer goin' to be fightin' on in the war.'

There was a short silence.

'War?' said Willy. 'What war? The Spanish one?'

'The one I'm declarin' on the Queen of England, of course,' said O'Brion. 'Frankly, I'm astonished that you could 'ave arsked such a dumb question.'

'Did he say he was declaring war on the Queen?' whispered Walden to Charlie.

'War?' said Elbows. 'He doesn't look like he'd be too much trouble for the Queen! He's just a silly old nutter!'

'Of course he is, Elbows,' hissed Charlie. 'But that's not the point!'

'Oh, right,' said Elbows. 'What is the point?'

'The point *is*,' said Walden, scratching his chin frantically, 'that, silly or not, if this character marches on Richmond Palace and the Queen gets wind of the fact that Yorick here is related to him, it would be the end of the palace gig. She knows Yorick's in the Black Skulls, and I bet she'd think we were mixed up in it somehow. We'd all be sent packing with no pay! Nothing at all!'

This was beginning to sound bad, Willy thought. Very bad.

'Walden, I hate to correct you,' said Charlie, 'but it'd be far worse than that. You know how the Queen feels about traitors. If she thought the Skulls were in league with O'Brion, she'd

lock us all in the Tower of London and throw away the key! We'd be there forever. It would be the end of England's most popular theatrical artistes!' He put his hand to his head and looked like he was going to pass out.

'We'll be lucky to escape with our lives!' said Minty.

'We've got to stop him, lads!' said Charlie. He paused and looked at Walden, a panicky expression on his face. 'We've got to make sure O'Brion doesn't go anywhere near to the palace!'

Walden nodded furiously.

Willy nodded even more furiously.

Charlie turned back to O'Brion and bowed. He smiled the same smile you might give someone who has told you they have married the man in the moon. 'Let me consult with my, um, associates, Your Highness,' he said.

Charlie herded the Skulls to the far side of the clearing. 'What are we going to do?' he hissed. 'If that raving loony gets anywhere near the Queen, it'll be the end of the Skulls! We'll all be in the Tower for the rest of our lives!'

'I don't want to go to the Tower,' said Willy. 'Anything would be better than that. Apart from going back to Stratford, of course!'

'Anything, eh?' said Charlie as he put a hand on Willy's shoulder. 'It just so happens that *you* might get to be a hero, Waggledagger!'

'Me?' said Willy.

'If someone was to pop over to the palace and get this belt back, O'Brion would have no reason to upset the Queen, would he?' Charlie said. 'Wouldn't you agree, Walden?'

'I would indeed, Charlie!' said Walden. 'Waggledagger could be the man of the hour, and no mistake!'

'Cut it out, you two,' said Yorick. 'Wot, exackly, do you want the boy to do? Steal the belt? Arsk 'Er Majesty if we can borrow it fer a bit? You can't send the boy on a mission like that, all on 'is own!'

Walden smiled. 'He won't be on his own, Yorick. You'll be going too. You've got to go to the palace anyway, to set up the stage.'

'Now look 'ere——' said Yorick.

'Why can't Minty go and get this belt?' interrupted Willy, 'or Elbows, or someone?'

Charlie leaned close to Willy. 'Can you really see Minty doing something as tricky as this? Or Olly? And you know Elbows! He's about as tricky as a brick. Walden and I can't go. We're needed to . . . erm . . . run things. You know, make sure everything works smoothly. Besides, you've just joined the Skulls. If you get caught pinching this belt, you're . . .' Charlie squinted at the sky, as if trying to think of the right word.

''E means that if you get caught stealin' the belt, the Skulls won't get the blame,' said Yorick. 'Ain't that right, Charlie?'

'Well, I wouldn't have put it *quite* like that, Yorick,' said Charlie, 'but it boils down to this: Waggledagger gets this belt from the Queen, or he ships out of the Skulls. One way or the other. We need to make sure that O'Brion doesn't go off half-cocked and invade the palace without telling us!'

'But ...' said Willy. He didn't want to steal anything, let alone something that belonged to the Queen of England. On the other hand, he didn't want the Skulls to spend the rest of their days in the Tower. And he *really* didn't want to go back to Stratford.

'No time to waste talking about details, Waggledagger,' said Charlie. He pasted his best oily smile onto his face and marched briskly up to O'Brion. Willy and Yorick followed him reluctantly.

'Begging your pardon, Your Majesty?' said Charlie.

O'Brion's goat came rather closer than

Charlie would have liked, and a crow landed on his head.

'Yes?' said O'Brion.

'Charlie Ginnell, Black Skulls manager,' said Charlie. 'I've been thinking. About this war. And the ... er ... the belt thing ...'

'The Golden Girdle.' O'Brion raised his bushy eyebrows. 'Wot of it?'

'Well, it's like this,' murmured Charlie, his voice pure velvet. 'I'm not sure it's a good idea for *you* to go to the palace directly at first. I think you should send someone else. There are plenty of bright lads in the Skulls who could go. Let *them* have a stab at getting the belt back without causing a lot of needless fuss. If they succeed, the Queen won't know it's missing. And even if they get caught, how could she know who sent them? They'll be the ones locked up in the Tower, and you'll still be free to plan your, er ... war from out here in the forest. What have you got to lose?'

O'Brion scratched the mouse in his beard thoughtfully. 'You may 'ave a point there, Mr Ginnell. Wot do I 'ave to lose?'

'Absolutely nothing,' said Charlie, nodding. 'So it's settled, then? Someone from the Skulls will go and retrieve the belt for you?'

The crow flew off and settled on Eric's head. Willy shuffled a bit nearer to the conversation.

'Very well,' said O'Brion.

Charlie sighed with relief.

'Let us try your plan first,' continued O'Brion. 'But there's still the little problem of the leprechauns.'

'Leprechauns?' said Willy. No one had told him anything about a possible leprechaun problem.

'Nasty little Irish devils,' said O'Brion. 'Bane of me life!' He eyed Charlie doubtfully. 'If some of your boys are goin' to the palace, those leprechauns will be sure to try and cause trouble,' he went on. 'Them fellers would love to get their greedy little hands on the Golden Girdle! I couldn't let you try and bring it back 'ere wivout protection.'

'I told you there were magical creatures in this wood, Yorick!' said Minty, scuttling up to peer over O'Brion's shoulder.

Yorick rolled his eyes and sighed.

O'Brion thrust a grimy hand deep into the folds of his robe, pulled out a large bottle and handed it to Willy. 'Love potion,' he said.

'That's not going to be much good,' said Minty. 'Haven't you got anything more useful?'

'Like a leprechaun-fightin' potion?' said O'Brion.

'Exactly,' said Minty.

'Don't be so ridiculous,' said O'Brion. 'Everyone knows leprechaun-fightin' potions take a long time to prepare *and* that one of the ingredients is rhinoceros toenails. Do you 'ave any idea 'ow 'ard it is to find one of those at short notice? Love potions are the best I can do jist now. You'll 'ave to make the most of it. One drop from this bottle and that leprechaun falls in love with the very next person he sees, got it?'

As the King of the Faeries spoke, the rest of the Skulls drew closer.

'Fall in love with anyone?' said Elbows. 'Even Yorick?'

The other Skulls tittered.

'That's right, actor,' said O'Brion. 'One drop: fall in love. If you wants to reverse it, give 'em a second drop. Easy.'

'It sounds complicated,' said Willy, giving the bottle a shake. He wasn't convinced that leprechauns even existed, but there was no doubting that O'Brion believed they did, and Willy wanted to stay on his good side.

'Careful, boy!' yelled O'Brion. 'One slip and that potion could hexplode all over us! Who knows wot might 'appen then!'

Yorick grabbed the bottle. 'I fink we'll manage,' he said. 'It's not like we're goin' to *use* the stuff, is it?' he muttered to Willy. Then he turned to Charlie. 'And don't fink you've got us nailed on fer that girdle business, either, Charlie Ginnell. We ain't stealin' *nuffink*!'

'*You two* are stealin' the Girdle?' said O'Brion, his ears perking up. 'Wot a great idea!'

Charlie beamed. 'I know!' he said.

'It ain't 'appening,' said Yorick, much to Willy's relief.

'Shame,' said O'Brion, a sly look coming over his face. ''Cos if I don't get me Girdle, before I go to war I might jist 'ave to spill the beans about that little story involving you, the miller's wife, the goose fat and the barrel of . . .'

Yorick staggered. 'You wouldn't, would you?' he whispered. 'Bruv?'

'Jist watch me,' said O'Brion.

'What story?' said Willy.

'Never you mind,' said Yorick quickly. 'We'll jist 'ave to get this flamin' belt.'

'Very well then,' said O'Brion sweetly. 'It's settled. You 'ave exackly one day to bring me the Golden Girdle, or I go war on the Queen and to 'eck wiv the consequences. Now I must be off, I 'ave an important meeting wiv the Council of Witches. Bit of an issue wiv the new type of broom.'

With that, the King of the Faeries turned and tippy-toed back into the forest.

The Skulls looked at Yorick.

Yorick glared at them. 'Not a word from any of you,' he growled. 'Not. A. Chuffing. Word.'

He picked up the frying pan Willy had thrown at the bush and slammed it down onto the embers of the fire.

'Right,' Yorick went on, 'any fool knows if there's proper work to be done, you needs a full belly. Willy, go and see wot you can scrounge up in the way of heggs.'

Willy opened up the store box on the back of the cart. A couple of eggs had broken and gone rotten.

Just like this trip.

5

Yorick and the Bolt of Cupid

Golden sunlight dappled the forest floor, and a passing lark trilled a song of joy that drifted through the clearing. *Tra-la-la-la.*

Willy looked for something to throw at it. A rock would do. Or a log. Why did stupid birds flap around singing stupid songs when it was obvious to anyone with half a brain that the world was a miserable place, full of horrible people (such as Charlie and Walden), getting nice people (such as Willy and Yorick), to do difficult and dangerous things (such as stealing the Queen's belt)?

Willy cracked an egg into the pan, and

flipped Yorick's bacon over. There was nothing, but nothing, that Yorick liked more than a fry-up. Willy knew that a Yorick operating on full capacity was exactly what he needed if they were to stand a chance of getting that stupid belt.

Ten minutes later, every last trace of Willy's Full English breakfast rested peacefully inside Yorick's stomach. Willy hitched Eric to the cart and the mission to the palace rumbled out of the clearing. The rest of the Skulls turned from their various tasks to watch them go.

As the first royal pennants of the palace appeared fluttering above the top of the trees, Willy's guts churned like a pond full of tadpoles in a hailstorm. He began to squirm in his seat.

'Relax,' said Yorick. 'They're all jist *people*, Waggledagger. No matter 'ow fancy they fink they are, they're all 'uman. Well, most of 'em, anyways.'

'I'm not worried about meeting *posh* people,

Yorick,' said Willy. 'I'm worried about getting caught stealing the Queen's golden belt! I'm not sure what the exact punishment is for that, but I'm pretty sure it will hurt.'

'Ah,' said Yorick, his face clouding over, 'the belt. Still, no point in worryin' about that jist yet, eh? We'll fink of summink, couple of bright sparks like us!'

Willy groaned. He didn't feel very sparky.

'Well, there she is,' said Yorick. 'Richmond Palace. Not too shabby.'

The place was big. Very big. The biggest building Willy had ever seen. And, flying proudly above its highest point, was the Queen's flag, telling the world that she was at home.

They pulled up at the main gate and a palace guard stepped forward. His gleaming sword and unsmiling face did nothing to calm Willy's nerves. Yorick explained their business and the guard directed them through the arched gate and into the courtyard.

Yorick tied Eric to a handy flagpole, and left him standing quietly between the shafts of the cart.

Willy looked around, his mouth hanging open. He had expected something quiet and hushed, like a library, except with soldiers instead of librarians. Richmond Palace was more like Stratford High Street on market day. There were people *everywhere*, hurrying to and fro. But that was where the resemblance ended.

For a start, everyone at the palace looked like a twerp. Black seemed to be the preferred choice of colour for the men's clothes. And very silly most of them looked, too, in their sweeping capes, puffed-out pantaloons, huge neck-choking ruffs, waistcoats embroidered with spangles, and shirts trimmed with the flounciest of French lace.

The ladies were dressed in shimmering silks and brocades, heaped layer upon layer until it was hard to see the person inside. The sun glinted off diamond necklaces wrapped around white-powdered throats and everywhere fingers dripped with gold.

It wasn't Stratford, that was certain.

''Scuse me, squire,' said Yorick, stopping a tall man dressed in a long purple gown and pointy hat. 'We're lookin' fer the Queen. Got a bit of a job on. Can you point us in the right direction, there's a good feller? Nice 'at, by the way.'

The man looked at Yorick in the same way you might look at an escaped bear you had discovered in your bedroom. After a moment's silence, he raised a white-gloved hand and pointed it in the direction of the inner gardens. 'I—I believe that Her Majesty is exercising the monarchical body corporeal by perambulating amidst the fruits of God's divine providence.'

'Eh?' said Yorick.

'He means she's in the garden,' said Willy.

'Well, why didn't 'e *say* so?' said Yorick, as he headed off in the direction the man had indicated. 'Fer a moment there I fort 'e'd got summink stuck in 'is mouth.'

'Don't you know who that was?' said Willy, following him.

'The Archbishop of Canterbury. Yes, I know, Waggledagger. But you can't blame me fer 'aving a bit o' fun wiv the old fraud, now, can you?'

They rounded a corner into the rose garden. Vast, overflowing beds of every sort of rose assaulted the eye and the nose. The Queen was in the centre of the garden, surrounded by flashily dressed lords and ladies. A pageboy hovered alongside the Queen, carrying a silver platter piled high with fruit and sweets. On her other side was another pageboy with another tray, upon which sat several goblets and a jug of wine.

As the Queen raised her hand to nibble on

a herb-encrusted swan-foot, her waistcoat shifted upwards and Willy caught a glimpse of something golden and gleaming tied tightly around her middle.

'Did you see that?' said Willy.

'Wot?' said Yorick.

'The belt! I think she's wearing it!'

Yorick grunted. 'Most likely,' he whispered. 'But there's not much we can do about it now, Waggledagger, is there? Too many witnesses, right? Keep yer powder dry fer now.'

Willy had only caught a glimpse of the girdle, but he had seen that it was made of smooth gold and was about the width of a man's hand. It was laced together with white ribbons and studded with precious gems. It looked magnificent. It looked expensive.

It looked impossible to separate from the Queen without her noticing.

Willy and Yorick shuffled through the chattering crowd, edging closer to the Queen.

Suddenly Willy realised someone was looking at him. It was a very large, extremely ugly Codpiece, one of the Queen's Royal Protection Squad. He was staring at Willy as if itching to test his dangerous-looking pike on Willy's neck.

'That Codpiece is looking at me funny, Yorick,' muttered Willy. 'I think it's one of the ones who were chasing me up in Stratford. I wonder if Codpieces bear grudges?'

'Get a grip, Waggledagger!' said Yorick. 'All that nonsense woz ironed out back in Stratford. The Queen likes us, remember? Wot are you, man or mouse?'

'Squeak?' said Willy.

Yorick was already shouldering his way towards the Queen. Willy hesitated as the Codpieces stared at him and began muttering to each other. It was all very well for Yorick to say that everything in Stratford had been ironed out, but what if that news hadn't got this far south? And from the look on the faces of these two specimens, it looked like that was exactly the case.

One of the Codpieces slipped around the back of a nearby hedge. The other pointed his pike at Willy in an alarming way. Willy shivered as a picture of his head sitting on top of that very pike sprang into his mind. He gulped. He didn't want anything to happen to his neck. He liked his neck. No, he *loved* his neck.

And that was when a tiny idea began to tickle the part of Willy's brain that came up with clever stuff.

Love.

That was it!

He plunged his hand inside his tunic and grabbed the bottle of love potion.

Supposing, just supposing, O'Brion was telling the truth! What if this stuff actually worked? And what if Willy somehow slipped a little potion to the Codpieces? They'd forget all about being horrible, nasty Codpieces and start being lovely, cuddly Codpieces. And, if the potion didn't work, then at least Willy would have tried *something*, right?

Willy gripped the bottle in his sweaty hand and followed Yorick as the last of the velvet-clad lords stepped aside.

Yorick took off his battered black hat and bowed deeply in front of the Queen. 'Beggin' yer pardon, Yer Majesty,' he said, 'but we've come to start settin' up fer yer play. We woz wonderin' where you wanted the stage to go, like?'

The royal party goggled at Yorick. It was as if one of the stone urns had grown legs and started speaking. The Queen's face was blank.

'The Black Skulls?' repeated Yorick. 'Actors? Singin'? Bit o' dancin'? Ringin' any bells?'

'Ah,' said the Queen, 'the Skulls, of course. One remembers the delightful little amusement you performed up at Vile's place. Too, too funny!' She chuckled lightly.

'HAHAHAHAHAHAHAHAHAHAHAHAHA!' screamed the lords and ladies in unison, squawking like a flock of seagulls. One or two slapped their knees. A small round baron turned as red as a raspberry and looked as though he might pass out from the sheer funniness of the royal remark.

Then the Queen stopped chuckling, and immediately everyone else did the same. The Codpieces eyed the nobles in confusion.

Willy sniffed a chance.

With everybody's attention fixed on the Queen and Yorick, Willy scuttled around the back of the royal party. He crept up behind the pageboy with the drinks and tapped him on one shoulder. When the boy turned to see who was there, Willy darted around to his other side and slopped some potion into the goblets on the tray. Then he ducked behind a fat nobleman in a long fur robe.

Now all he had to do was make sure the

Codpieces drank the potion. *And* hope that it worked.

The Queen and Yorick were still talking.

'One thought the ballroom might make a suitable venue for your play,' said the Queen.

'A fine choice, Ma'am,' said Yorick, 'if I may be so bold. Now if I could . . .'

Willy sidled up to the pageboy again. 'Begging your pardon, page,' he whispered. 'But I heard one of the Codpieces saying that they were thirsty enough to drink the Thames dry. Why, one of them said he was so thirsty he might get a sudden urge to slay a page or two. I'd get a move on, if I were you.'

The pageboy almost dropped the tray in his fright.

'It was the really ugly one who said it,' added Willy.

'Egbert Stott?' gasped the page. 'He's the meanest of 'em all!'

The pageboy headed towards the Codpiece

called Stott. Unfortunately, his path took him directly past Yorick.

''Scuse, me, Yer Majesty,' said Yorick, breaking off to grab a goblet from the passing page. 'I'm absolutely parched!'

He raised the goblet to his lips.

'Wait!' shouted Willy.

It was too late.

Yorick took a deep swig from the goblet and handed it back to the pageboy. 'That 'it the spot an' no mistake, Yer 'Iyhness.'

The Queen raised an uninterested royal eyebrow. 'You are dismissed,' she said as, with a rustling of satin and brocade, she began gliding royally towards the palace.

Yorick didn't move.

He was standing bolt upright, with an expression on his face that reminded Willy of the look Yorick got just before one of his extra-stinky botty burps.

Please, thought Willy, let it only be a fart.

A fart, even in front of the Queen, he could cope with. But if O'Brion was right about the love potion . . .

O'Brion was.

''As anyone ever told you,' cried Yorick, scampering to catch up with the Queen, 'that you 'ave eyes like twin sapphires and lips like a sunrise in summer?' His voice had gone soft and soppy. 'Or that yer skin is as smooth as finest marble?'

Willy groaned. The potion really did work.

The only trouble was, the wrong person had taken it.

The Queen halted in mid-saunter. She frowned and pursed her lips. 'Twin sapphires?' she said. 'That's very sweet of you, actor person. But you are rather large, and scruffy and *common*. For all one knows, you might even be *dangerous*.'

Egbert Stott growled. The other Codpiece shuffled towards Yorick with a mean gleam in his eye. They seemed to have forgotten about Willy for the moment, but that didn't make Willy feel any better.

Lord Melonsquidger, one of the Queen's courtiers, tittered loudly.

Yorick pulled a fistful of roses from a nearby flowerbed and thrust them at the Queen. 'Flowers fer the sweetest flower of all,' he said with a hideous smile.

Willy was almost sick.

'Er, thank you, one supposes, odd peasant person,' said the Queen, passing the flowers to Lord Melonsquidger.

'Let us dance till dawn!' trilled Yorick, grabbing the Queen's hand.

'Oi!' shouted Stott. 'No touchin' of the Royal Person!' He lunged forward and jabbed the point of his pike under Yorick's throat.

Yorick, love spell or not, knew when to back down.

'A fousand rose-covered apologies, Yer

Royal Loveliness!' he said, bowing. 'I woz jist overcome! Overcome wiv love, my Lady. Love, I tells you!' He spun around and started performing what could only be described as a jig. 'I shall dance to show you me true feelins!'

Yorick leapt around, looking as though he was attempting to get a ferret out of his undergarments.

Willy racked his brains, trying to remember what O'Brion had said about the love potion. Did a second dose *reverse* the effects? If so, all Willy had to do was get Yorick to take another swig from one of the goblets.

He headed for the pageboy who held the tray. As he did so, a jab from Stott's pike sent Yorick stumbling backwards. Yorick barged into Lady Hippolyta Roundbottom, knocking her straight into a rosebush. Then he bounced heavily towards the pageboy with the drinks.

Willy darted forwards through a thicket of flouncy skirts and pantaloons, and grabbed the tray, just as Yorick came crashing down on top of the page.

'Just in time!' said Willy.

With the ladies distracted by the screams coming from beneath Yorick, and the lords trying to hoist Lady Hippolyta from the rose-bush, Willy steered his way towards Yorick.

Yorick peered up at Stott. 'No need to get nasty,' he said. 'I woz only dancin' me dance of love.'

'*Hellllllp meeeeeeeeee*,' came a muffled cry from somewhere south of Yorick's bottom.

'Sorry, me old mucker,' said Yorick getting slowly to his feet. 'I do apologise.'

'*Uuuuuuuurgh*,' groaned the pageboy.

Yorick looked around for the Queen.

Egbert Stott stepped forwards with his pike. 'I told you,' he said, 'no one touches 'Er Majesty!'

'I wozn't touchin' 'er!' cried Yorick.

'The hairy commoner *is* being jolly

pleasant,' said the Queen. 'Lower your pike, Codpiece.' It had been a very long time since anyone told her that her lips resembled a sunrise.

'Here,' hissed Willy, shoving the tray of drinks under Yorick's nose. 'Drink this!'

'Oh, fanks, Waggledagger,' said Yorick. 'I'd forgotten you woz 'ere.' He raised the goblet to his lips.

Suddenly a blast from a hunting horn ripped through the rose garden.

'Drink!' hissed Willy.

Distracted, Yorick replaced the goblet on the tray. The hunting horn blew again. A group of sweaty toffs dressed in hunting gear swaggered into the garden. They carried an extraordinary number of dead birds. At the head of the group was a familiar figure.

Sir Victor Vile.

Willy's shoulders slumped. If he were to draw up a list of people he'd least like to see ever again, Sir Victor would have been near the top. Yet there he was, striding towards the Queen, a smug smile plastered upon his normally crabby face.

Sir Victor bowed graciously.

'Vile,' said the Queen. 'Been hunting again, I see.'

'As usual, Your Majesty, nothing escapes your eagle eye,' said Sir Victor. 'Good grief!' he sputtered, catching sight of Willy. 'The revolting Stratford boy! What are you doing here?'

''Er Majesty,' said Yorick, 'woz kind enough to arsk us to perform 'ere at the palace, if Yer Lordship recalls.'

Sir Victor scowled. 'Ah, yes, I remember now.' He glared at Willy. 'And I certainly haven't forgotten the trouble *you* caused, you half-formed little weevil. I've got my beady eye on you!'

He turned and bowed again to the Queen,

the smarmy smile back on his face. 'And now, Madam, I will away to make myself more presentable for your court. This hot weather has parched my throat and dusted my person enough.'

Before Willy could move, the Queen snatched a goblet from the tray and handed it to Sir Victor. 'Here, Vile,' she said. 'Perhaps this will help you on your way.'

'You are too kind, Your Majesty!' said Sir Victor. 'Just what I need on a day such as this! I bid you farewell, my Lady!' He raised the goblet to his lips and drained it before tossing it carelessly over his shoulder.

Willy said nothing. There was nothing to say.

6

Blind Cupid

Willy knew what would happen next. Sir Victor would fall in love with the Queen. The idea of Sir Victor as King of England didn't bear thinking about. To say nothing of how Yorick would react if he discovered Sir Victor was a love rival.

There was only one thing to do.

Before Sir Victor had a chance to so much as blink in the Queen's direction, Willy lunged forward, yanked the brim of Sir Victor's hunting hat down over his eyes and pushed him away from the Queen.

Sir Victor slammed headlong into the group

of courtiers. They skittled aside like so many overdressed squealing ninepins.

Egbert Stott leapt straight on top of the Queen, knocking her to the floor. 'Code Red!' he yelled, his pike at the ready for Spanish spies, Scottish warlords, and other would-be assassins.

Sir Victor scrambled to his feet, his hat crammed over his face. 'By Zeus!' he cried. 'What dunderheaded villainy is this?' He seized hold of his hat and began to pull.

After a second or two of loud swearing, the hat popped off, and Sir Victor blinked straight into the eyes of Lady Hippolyta Roundbottom. 'Good day, Madam,' he said politely.

Then, quite suddenly, as if he'd been coshed across the back of the neck with a jumbo-sized black pudding, Sir Victor jerked to one side and a dazed look drifted across his face. He turned back to Lady Hippolyta, a dopey smile on his face.

'Good day, Your Lordship,' said Lady Hippolyta.

'Y-y-your eyes,' stammered Sir Victor. 'Has anyone ever t-t-told you they are like pools of bluest sapphires set in a coral sea?'

No one, not even her mother, would have described Lady Hippolyta's eyes in that way. There was only one of them, for a start, the other having been lost long ago in a nasty accident involving a lemon. She also had a number of highly-polished wooden teeth sprinkled here and there in her mouth. These choppers, which looked like they might be rather difficult to use, clearly worked just fine when it came to eating. Lady Hippolyta was roughly the size of a baby elephant.

Willy, still cluching the tray of drinks, watched in horror. His simple plan was quickly becoming a Grade-A disaster. The only good thing was that everyone seemed to have forgotten that Willy was the one who had manhandled Sir Victor in the first place.

Lady Hippolyta smiled, displaying a varied collection of spinach and greyish meat caught between her wooden teeth.

'How is it I have not noticed you before, m'Lady?' purred Sir Victor. He waggled his moustache.

Lady Hippolyta giggled. Her laugh had all the tinkling beauty of a cat being squeezed in a mangle. She pushed Sir Victor playfully, sending him staggering backwards. 'You are a smooth one, Sir Victor!' she said. Then she lifted a fan to her face and fluttered it furiously, batting her one good eyelid over the top.

There was a muffled squeak from somewhere underneath Egbert Stott. He lifted a section of his belly and the Queen's head poked out.

'Get *off* me, you imbecile!' she hissed. 'At once!'

Egbert Stott got to his feet and pulled the

Queen upright. 'Very sorry, Ma'am, I'm sure,' he said. 'But you can't be too careful when there are spies around.'

The Queen shot him a withering glare, before turning to Lady Hippolyta. 'And what, pray, has got into you, my Lady?' she barked.

'It is love, Madam!' gushed Sir Victor. 'The lady is the object of my love!'

'*Love?*' said the Queen. 'Have you banged your head, Vile?'

Sir Victor fell to one knee and took Lady Hippolyta's hand in his own. 'If I have, Your Majesty,' he said, 'it has only made my mind clearer. I wish to marry this angel.'

'A wedding!' Lord Melonsquidger exclaimed excitedly from behind the Queen's left shoulder. 'How simply *thrilling*!'

'Marry?' said the Queen. 'Are you sure?'

Sir Victor rubbed his chin and blinked. 'Yes I am, Your Majesty.'

'How exciting!' The Queen clapped her

hands and jumped up and down. There was nothing she liked better than a good wedding. Apart from a really good execution.

Willy tugged on Yorick's belt. 'Come on, Yorick,' he hissed. 'We'll have to forget about the belt for now. Let's get Eric and get out of here!'

'Go?' said Yorick, a puzzled look on his face. 'Wot do I want to go fer, when the love of me life is right 'ere?' And with that, he lunged in the direction of the Queen, but accidentally barged into Sir Victor on the way.

'Blast your eyes, you clumsy oaf!' cried Sir Victor, his sword already halfway out of its scabbard. 'Watch yourself or you'll get a taste of my steel!'

Yorick retreated a step, and Sir Victor turned back towards Lady Hippolyta. 'Did my lickle poochie get scared by the nasty peasant?' he trilled. 'And will my ickle hunny-bunny mawwy her big flopsy? *Hmm? Hmm?*'

'I will!' yelled Lady Hippolyta. She crushed Sir Victor to her gigantic bosom.

'Hurrah!' The Queen raised her royal hand in the air. 'This calls for a celebration! One decrees that the wedding between Sir Victor Vile and Lady Hippolyta will take place in the forest in two days' time, after which the Black Skulls will entertain one most royally. One shall have a real summer knees-up!'

There was a chorus of cheers.

The Queen grabbed hold of a goblet from the silver tray. 'To love!' she cried and drained the contents. She licked her lips and handed the goblet to the nearest person.

Egbert Stott.

The Queen glanced at him and then, just like Sir Victor before her, a stunned expression crept over her face. 'You, Codpiece person,' she murmured. 'What's your name?'

'Egbert, Your Majesty,' said Egbert. 'Egbert Stott.'

'Has anyone ever told you that you have hair like ripe corn, lips of cherry, and the physique of a Greek god?'

'Er, not lately, Your Majesty,' said Egbert. 'In fact, never.'

'Well, you have, you darling little common person!' purred the Queen. She ran a thin white finger down the front of Egbert's tunic and smiled up at him.

Willy did what any normal person would have done in the circumstances. He walked across the lawn to a small tree and began banging his forehead against the trunk.

almost faerie Time

'What a *disaster*,' said Willy as they headed slowly back to camp. 'Everyone's falling in love. And with the wrong people! You know what this means, don't you, Yorick?'

'Wot?' said Yorick, absent-mindedly. He appeared to be busy trying to compose a love song in his head.

'I'm getting very close to becoming an ex-Black Skull!' Willy wailed.

'You fink you've got problems,' growled Yorick. 'My sweetheart, the most beautifullest woman in all of England, is in love wiv a blinkin' Codpiece!'

Willy frowned. It was worse than he'd thought. Something would have to be done. He took the bottle of love potion out of his tunic. 'Yorick,' he said.

'Wot?' said Yorick gloomily.

'You do know you're only in love with the Queen because you drank some of O'Brion's potion, don't you? If you have another drop, the spell will be broken. Have a tiny sip now, and things will start looking up for both of us.'

Yorick's face went purple. ''Ow dare you, Waggledagger!' he said. 'Belittlin' this most glorious love of mine like that! Everybody knows me bruvver is barmy. No potion 'e makes could possibly work! Stands to reason! No, I've finally come to me senses, that's all, and realised I can't live anuvver day wivout 'Er 'Ighness's beautiful royal personage in me life!'

'But, Yorick!' said Willy.

'That's *enough*!' said Yorick. 'I'll 'ear no more nonsense from you about potions!'

Willy sighed. He knew when he was beaten. He'd have to find another way to get Yorick back to his old self. He gave up trying to convince Yorick to take the potion, and flapped Eric's reins.

Not that he was in any hurry to get back. 'What are we going to tell O'Brion about the belt?' he asked. 'And Charlie and Walden? What are *they* going to say? Now the Queen wants the play in the forest. They're not going to be very happy about that!'

Yorick thrust out his lower lip and nodded. 'No, they ain't, that's fer sure. And yer right about me loopy bruv, too. 'E will do 'is nut, Waggledagger. 'E might even wage war on me precious Queen, and then I'll 'ave to challenge 'im to a duel, and then where will we be?'

'Oh thanks for that, Yorick,' said Willy. 'You've really cheered me up.'

*

Back at the clearing, the Skulls had been spending the morning brushing up on their acts. No one was pleased with Willy and Yorick's news.

'Here?' said Minty Macvelli, putting down the joke book he had been studying. 'We have to perform our new play out here in the woods?'

'Maybe it's not so b——' said Willy.

'It's outrageous!' cried Olly, who had been practising his best winning smile in a mirror. He stamped his black leather boots. 'I am a professional actor!'

'But, you've performed outside befo——' Willy said.

'And O'Brion's darn belt?' hissed Charlie. He threw down the accounts book he'd been poring over and shoved his face close to Willy's. 'I don't suppose you've got that either, have you?'

'I did see it around the Queen's wai——' said Willy.

'Oh lovely Queenie,' warbled Yorick. 'Don't be such a meanie ...' He was sitting on a tree stump on the opposite side of the clearing, tunelessly strumming on a lute.

'What happened back there, Waggledagger?' wailed Walden, coming to stand next to Charlie. 'What on earth have you done to Yorick?'

'It wasn't my fault,' said Willy. 'Please don't send me back to Stratford! It was O'Brion's stupid love potion.'

Right on cue, the King of the Faeries lolloped out of the woods, followed by his troupe of grubby animals and flies. 'Well?' he shouted. 'Did you get it?'

'We didn't ...' said Willy. 'The Queen ... that is ... what I mean is ...'

'They haven't got your belt just yet, Your Majesty,' said Charlie smoothly. 'But thanks to our daring duo, the Queen is ...'

O'Brion's face darkened.

At that moment, Yorick came drifting past crooning something about moons in June. Then he wandered off towards the trees.

'I'm sorry about the belt, Mr King of the Faeries,' said Willy, quickly. 'But, about your love potion——'

'Never mind that!' snapped O'Brion. 'The Queen? You were sayin'?'

'She's coming here,' said Willy.

'She'll be here the day after tomorrow,' said Walden 'We'll be sure to get your belt for you then.'

'I 'opes so, Bogglebritches, or wotever yer name is,' O'Brion said. 'I wants that Girdle and I wants it now!'

Before Willy could say anything else, Yorick burst through the trees and trotted across the clearing.

'*You're so dreamy, Queenie, you're so creamy, Queenie, you're no in-betweenie, Queenie . . .*' sang Yorick, before crashing back into the woods.

'Wot's up wiv 'im, then?' said O'Brion. ''E don't seem 'is usual self.'

'He's not,' said Willy. 'He's in love. With the Queen.' He waved the love potion under O'Brion's nose. 'It works.'

''Course it works,' said O'Brion. 'I made it! But why'd you waste it on me bruvver?'

'It's a long story,' said Willy.

The rest of the Black Skulls, who'd been keeping a safe distance from O'Brion, suddenly pricked up their ears. They moved a few steps closer to where he stood with Willy, Charlie and Walden.

'Hey, you don't suppose the Queen would actually *go* for Yorick do you?' said Olly. 'What if he becomes *King* Yorick?'

'Don't even joke about that,' said Minty, closing his eyes and leaning against a cart for support.

'I don't think he's her type at the moment,' said Willy. 'She's, erm, in love with someone else.' He turned to O'Brion and held up the bottle. 'How long does it last?'

'I told you before, it lasts until you give 'im anuvver drop,' said O'Brion.

'But he's refusing to take it!' Willy said in despair.

'If I were you, I'd be more worried about the side heffects,' said O'Brion.

'What side effects?' said Willy. 'You never said anything about side effects.'

O'Brion opened his mouth to explain, but, before he had a chance, Yorick burst out of the woods with an idiotic grin on his face. He was playing a sickly love song on a set of wooden pipes. Wild flowers were woven through his hair. He took the pipes from his mouth and smiled madly, showing a gleaming set of yellow teeth. Shiny wings fluttered from his shoulders and his lower half had taken on the appearance of a donkey.

It wasn't a good look.

'Those side heffects,' said O'Brion, pointing. 'See the donkey's bottom? That's because love makes asses out of all! Them wings are Yorick's wings of love! They'll 'elp him fly all the quicker to 'is betrothed! The teeth I can't hexplain.'

At the sight of Yorick, the Black Skulls did what they did best. They panicked.

'Yorick's turned into a half-man, half-donkey monster!' yelled Charlie.

'He'll kick us to death!' shouted Walden.

'Run for your lives!' screamed Olly and dived into a half-empty barrel of spicy pickled otter's noses.

'Sweet Mary Mintballs!' yelled Elbows. 'It's an apparition!' He crossed himself and, picking up his fiddle, legged it into the trees on the opposite side of the clearing.

Minty, with Minimac in tow, leapt onto the driving board of the cart and cracked Eric's reins. 'Gee up, you big fur ball!' he yelled.

Eric turned his head, gave Minty a look of recognition and dumped a load of ox poop on the ground. Then he faced the front again and closed his eyes. Minty jumped off the cart and headed after Elbows. 'Wait for me and Minimac!' he yelled, as he crashed through a stand of ferns.

Within seconds, only O'Brion and Willy remained in the clearing (unless you counted the squirrel, the ox, and an assortment of bugs). Yorick clip-clopped his way towards them on his donkey hooves, the light of love shining brightly in his eyes.

'Why aren't you scared, Wibblewobble?' said O'Brion. 'Flee, while you 'ave a chance!'

Willy pointed at Yorick's legs. 'Those are the back legs of Dobbin, the Black Skulls pantomime horse. And the wings are just tied on with a bit of string, just like your . . .'

O'Brion's eyes narrowed. 'Yes? Wot about me wings?'

'Oh, um, nothing,' said Willy.

Yorick danced around the camp fire in time to the tootling of his wooden pipes. 'Tiptop mornin'!' he shouted. 'I woz dancin' a carefree jig of joy in the forest, when it came to me in a blindin' flash that I am none other than Pan, the forest god of love, or summink!'

'Doesn't Pan have the legs of a goat?' asked Willy.

Yorick waved his pipes airily. 'Goat, 'orse, wotever. They all got 'ooves, ain't they? Now, if you don't mind, I 'ave a love poem to compose.' He produced a bottle of ink and a sheet of parchment from some deep pocket in the pantomime horse's legs and settled down on the back of a cart. He wore a frown of deep concentration.

'This is downright embarrassin',' said the King of the Faeries.

'I know,' said Willy, miserably. 'If only you hadn't given me that stupid love potion . . .'

'I said to use it on the *leprechauns!*' snapped O'Brion. 'No, young Hogglediddler, this is *your* mess, fair an' square. 'Ow you sort it out ain't up to me. All I care about is me Girdle. You'd better get it back sharpish once the Queen arrives, or it's war!'

And with a last regal wave of the hand and an adjustment of his wings, O'Brion tiptoed his clod-hopping way out of the clearing.

After a few moments, Charlie emerged from the woods and peered at Yorick. 'All clear?' he said.

'I think so,' said Willy. 'Yorick isn't turning into a donkey, if that's what you're worried about.'

Suddenly Yorick jumped off the cart and patted his stomach. 'Got any grub?' he said. 'I'm famished!'

Willy almost fell over with relief. This was more like the old Yorick.

Charlie clearly thought the same. He put

two fingers in his mouth and whistled loudly. The rest of the Black Skulls began to emerge from their hiding places. They approached Yorick cautiously and assembled at the back of one of the carts.

'Is Donkey Boy safe?' said Minty, keeping Minimac as far away from Yorick as possible.

'It's a costume,' said Willy. 'Of course he's safe.'

'Put the doll away before I eats it,' said Yorick.

'Just as rude as ever, I see,' said Minimac. 'You must be feeling better.'

'Nice pants, Yorick,' said Elbows.

Charlie clambered onto the back of the cart. 'All right, settle down. We've wasted enough time on this "love" business,' he said, staring hard at Willy. 'We'll have to hope Waggledagger gets O'Brion's belt off the Queen as soon as she gets here, or it's the Tower for us, and back to Sunny Stratford for him!'

The Black Skulls nodded in agreement.

'In the meantime, we've got to do what the Black Skulls do best: perform!' Charlie continued. 'We've only got two days and we need every second. Walden, you're going to finish off that play. Something romantic, light, fluffy. None of your gloomy Danish rubbish. And get a character into the play who looks like the Queen, right? The royals love seeing themselves up there onstage. Waggledagger here can play her role: he's about the same height.'

'Right you are, Charlie,' said Walden.

Charlie turned to the others. 'Elbows, you sort out the music. I'm thinking jigs, reels, *happy* music. You know the sort of thing. Olly, you and Minty get the costumes sorted. Lots of white, ribbons, sparkly stuff. Use Elbows for any tricky bits of jewellery; you know he's good with all that sort of thing. Yorick and Waggledagger will fix up the stage area. Any questions?'

Olly pointed at Yorick. 'He's not going to try and kiss me or something, is he?' he said.

'You should be so lucky,' growled Yorick. He laced his fingers together and cracked his knuckles. It sounded like musket shot. 'It's true me 'eart belongs to the Queen, and I shall soon be leavin' you all and followin' 'er to the end of the earf, if she so desires. But the fact is, she arrives 'ere in the forest the day after tomorrow to see the play of a lifetime, and I 'ave a much bigger chance of himpressin' 'er wiv me skills, if she sees wot a wonderful stage-builder I am! So quit standin' around like a spare plank, Waggledagger, and let's get this show on the road!'

8
The Revels Out of Hand

It didn't take long for the Black Skulls to get back in the groove. It was soon clear to them that Yorick had *not* turned into some kind of woodland sprite. And with him bellowing orders, the little glade was transformed into something that resembled a theatre in no time at all.

Within a few hours, it was time for a run-through, and Minty was fastening Willy into his queen costume. The rest of the Skulls came to watch.

'Willy looks a lot like her,' said Minty, standing back to admire his handiwork.

'Not bad, for an amateur,' said Minimac

from his perch on top of a prop box.

'*One is most amused,*' squeaked Willy, in a queenly voice.

'Sounds like her too,' said Elbows.

'About time he did something useful!' said Charlie.

'I still think I would have made a much better Queen,' said Olly and stalked off towards his dressing tent.

Willy wished he could have enjoyed getting ready for his first onstage role. But if O'Brion and Yorick and the Queen weren't sorted out, all of Willy's friends could be in the Tower, and Willy himself could be back at home within a week. Just thinking about it made Willy's blood turn to ice.

'We'll easily have everything ready inside two days!' yelled Charlie above the sound of Yorick's hammer.

'Just as long as nothing else goes wrong,' muttered Walden, scribbling away.

'Ha!' said Charlie. 'What could possibly go wrong?'

There was a blast of trumpets in the distance.

'Was that you, Yorick?' said Willy.

'Not me,' said Yorick, his voice muffled by the mouthful of nails he had clenched in his teeth. 'Me bottom will be silent for as long as me love doth flourish.'

'That's an unexpected bonus,' said Elbows.

The trumpet sounded again. Then—with a clip-clop of hooves, a jangle of swords, the crunch of boots, and the high-pitched chatter that only a large number of posh people all talking at once can make—a royal procession clattered into the clearing. It was led by two Codpieces on prancing horses. The Queen rode behind them on a white steed.

'Oi, Waggledagger,' hissed Charlie. 'You'd best scoot out of sight while you're dressed up like that. The Queen might not like it.'

Willy hoicked up his skirts and legged it into one of the dressing tents, just as the Queen's trumpeter gave one last ear-splitting fanfare and the royal party pulled up. The Queen dismounted from her horse, and soon Sir Victor, Lady Hippolyta, Egbert Stott, the Archbishop of Canterbury, an assortment of Codpieces and several lords and ladies-in-waiting were all standing around in the clearing.

Yorick, still dressed in his Pan costume, was balanced high on a wooden hoist at the back of the stage. When he saw the Queen, he almost swallowed his mouthful of nails. He managed to spit them out, but promptly fell backwards off the hoist, knocking himself out cold. He rolled, unnoticed, under the stage.

'This looks like trouble,' muttered Charlie. He put down the page of script he'd been reading and trotted towards the Queen. 'Your Majesty!' he trilled, bowing as low as his huge stomach would allow. 'What a lovely surprise!

And I believe that congratulations are in order? Love is in the air, eh?'

The Queen blushed under her thick white make-up. 'And here one was, hoping to be the first to let you know!' she said.

Charlie started to wink and then remembered his manners. He wasn't sure if it was rude to wink at a monarch. For all he knew, it might be a hanging offence. 'I have my spies,' he said instead, putting a hand to the side of his mouth.

'Spies?' cried Egbert Stott. He leapt forward and thrust his pike at Charlie. 'Did someone say spies?'

'Do put down that pike, Egbert, my dear.' The Queen waved a finger at Stott and kissed his spotty nose. 'This, Mr Ginnell, is one's beloved. And just this morning, one has decided that Mr Stott here is the man who will become one's King! We are to be married. I say, are you all right, Mr Ginnell?'

Charlie was coughing uncontrollably. 'My c-c-congratulations, Your Majesty,' he spluttered. 'But I couldn't help but notice that Mr Stott is—how can I put this?—wearing a wedding ring. Is he already married to someone else?'

The Queen turned to the Archbishop and smiled. 'Indeed he is. Which is why one has brought along old Bertram here. One will leave him to fix all that. He did it for Daddy, after all!'

The Archbishop bared his teeth in what might have been a smile.

Egbert Stott blinked. There the Queen went again, banging on about getting married. His wife, Mrs Stott, wasn't going to like this. Mrs Stott's temper was bad enough when Egbert tracked his muddy boots across her kitchen floor. What Mrs Stott would say when she found out Egbert was marrying the Queen, he didn't like to imagine.

Willy, back in his own clothes, noticed O'Brion poke his leaf-entangled head out from a bush and peer intently at the Queen.

'*Psst!*' hissed O'Brion. 'Woggledoggle! You didn't say the Queen woz comin' *today*. 'Ave you got me Girdle yet?'

'Not as yet, Your Majesty,' said Willy. 'But we're working on it! Maybe you should stay hidden until we have something to tell you.'

'Very well,' O'Brion said. 'But I ain't waitin' around ferever, mind! Better 'urry up if you don't want that war.'

And with that he was gone.

Willy wiped his brow. He headed towards where the Queen was beginning a speech.

'You must all be wondering why one is here,' she said. 'It is because one has the most wonderful news! Sir Vile's wedding to Lady H will now be brought forward to tomorrow morning, and—more importantly—*one will join them by marring Mr Stott at the same time*!

Isn't that splendid? One has decided that there's no point in waiting. Love is love, after all! So, Mr Ginnell, if you'd be good enough to jolly your play along a bit faster, one will come back in the morning for a lovely wedding!' She glanced at Sir Victor and Lady Hippolyta. 'Or two!' she added.

Charlie turned a nasty shade of green. 'Two weddings?' he hissed to Walden. 'And a finished play? *By tomorrow morning?*'

Walden was making little moaning noises. 'Impossible!' he whispered. 'We'll never do it!'

'Impossible isn't a word the Queen is used to hearing,' said Charlie. He elbowed Walden to one side and bowed. 'Not the teensiest tiniest problem, Your Majesty.'

'Capital!' said the Queen. 'Now, one would like everyone to join one in a toast! A toast to love! But before that, the Archbishop would like to say a few words of his own.'

The two pageboys trotted forward with their

usual trays of goblets and jugs of wine. They placed them on a flat tree stump and stood back.

The Archbishop drew in a long and wavering breath. ''Tis a most wondrous miracle to behold,' he quavered. 'The miracle of love! And when that miracle is embodied in the very . . .'

As the Archbishop droned on, Willy noticed O'Brion's head pop up out of the bushes again. O'Brion mimed placing a belt around his waist, and pointed towards the Queen. Willy nodded and made a gesture that was meant to let O'Brion know that he, Willy Waggledagger, had it all sorted out, and it would only be a matter of time before he managed to wangle the Golden Girdle away from the Queen of England. It was a lot to say with only one gesture.

'What are you doing, Waggledagger?' said Charlie, sidling over and grabbing Willy by the arm. 'You look like you've got a spider in your undercrackers!'

'I——' said Willy, but got no further.

Charlie shook a pudgy finger in Willy's face. 'You've no time to waste jigging about like a demented baboon, boy!' he hissed. 'This is all your fault, giving everyone that stupid love potion! All we'll have ready are some half-finished scenes and a couple of costumes! As for that idiot O'Brion, he'll declare war unless he gets that flaming belt soon! We must buy some time! Think of something, or you're *out*!' he finished, and stormed off.

In the background the Archbishop was still burbling away. 'Most wondrous of monarchs! Most beauteous of Queens! Most . . .'

The Queen stifled a yawn.

Willy didn't hear a word. The only sound he could hear was the echo of Charlie's words ringing in his ears: *'you're out . . . you're out . . . you're out'*. His short and not very glorious

career as a Black Skull looked like it was over almost before it had begun. He turned and trudged back to the carts. He might as well pack his bag right away. There was no point waiting for the morning.

As Willy pulled together his few meagre belongings and stuffed them into a sack, his mind ran over everything that had happened to him since he'd met the Skulls. Admittedly, some of those things were pretty horrible, like the time he'd had to hide from Sir Victor under Yorick's snotty handkerchief, or the time that craggy old witch had put her finger up his nose.

But mostly, Willy had had the time of his life. Willy would miss the feeling he got when, after a long hard day on the road, the Skulls gathered around the camp fire and sang songs, or told stories about actors and theatres, about great performances and howlingly bad ones. Willy never had much to say at these times but, for the first time in his life, he felt like he really belonged somewhere.

But that was over now. Willy had been given the chance of a lifetime, and what had he done? He'd blown it. As usual. Thanks to his stupid idea with the love potion, everyone would probably be locked in the Tower of London by tomorrow. It would be best if he just left now, before he made everything worse than it already was.

With a sigh, he slung his sack of belongings over his shoulder and trudged off into the shade of the forest, following the track that would eventually lead him back to Stratford.

He'd just have to make the best of it, even though he could already picture his father's smug grin and thick belt waiting for him back home.

Maybe if he promised to wash the tanning-room floor and clean out all the vats of animal innards every day from now until he was twenty-one, his father would forgive him . . .

Willy shook his head. Who was he trying to kid? There'd be fireworks at the Shakespeare house when he got back, and no mistake.

Suddenly, Willy stopped dead in his tracks.

Fireworks.

That was it.

He dropped his sack of belongings to the ground and trotted back to the camp as fast as he could.

As Willy rounded the back of the stage, his left foot clipped something that lay on the ground. He tripped and sprawled onto the grass. Picking himself up, he bent down to examine the object that had tripped him. It was a pantomime horse's hoof, poking out from beneath the stage.

The hoof was attached to a leg. Willy took hold of the leg and pulled as hard as he could. After three mighty heaves, the unconscious form of Yorick rolled out onto the grass.

'Yorick!' shouted Willy, giving the big man a shake. 'Wake up! I've got an idea!'

9

MEDDLING MONKEYS

'Why do you need a diversion?' mumbled a dazed and confused Yorick.

'I just need one,' said Willy. 'Trust me.'

Yorick rubbed his head. A bump the size of a heron's egg was visible just below his hairline. 'It might upset the Queen,' he said. 'A great loud noise like wot you're suggestin'. No, I couldn't do that to the woman wot I am goin' to marry!' Yorick pointed to the Archbishop. 'Wot's 'e goin' on about now?'

'He's been talking like that for ages,' said Willy. He took a deep breath. He was going to have to break Yorick's heart. There was no other way. 'You do know that the Queen is going to *marry* that Egbert Stott, don't you, Yorick?' he said gently.

'Marry! That slab-faced plug-ugly Codpiece!' gasped Yorick.

'Yes,' Willy said. 'The wedding's tomorrow.'

Yorick staggered and clutched his chest. 'Oh woe! Oh fie! Such betrayal! I'm gonna rip 'is gizzard out!'

'Or we could try my plan,' said Willy. 'The one with the diversion?'

'Will this plan prevent me beloved makin' an 'orrible mistake and marryin' that revoltin' twerp?' said Yorick.

'I hope so,' said Willy.

'Then stand back, Waggledagger, and wait fer a diversion, the likes of which ain't never been seen in all the realm!' thundered Yorick. He darted off in the direction of the carts. 'Two minutes and then it all goes off! Right?' he said over his shoulder.

Willy nodded and headed for the pageboys who, like everyone else, were waiting for the Archbishop's ramblings to grind to a halt.

On the other side of the clearing, Yorick retrieved one of his special-effects flashpots from its place near the cooking fire and set off into the woods.

Willy tried to look invisible as he crept closer to the pageboys' goblets. It was quite easy, as everyone had their eyes fixed firmly on the Archbishop. It would have been very impolite to be seen to have stopped listening to him, no matter how boring he was.

'And so, brethren,' said the Archbishop as he approached the finish line, 'it is with most lustrous marvellitude and phantasmagorical gratitude that I congratulate Her Most Glorious Majesty and ... er ... Mr Stott on their impending nuptials!'

There was a general sigh of relief and a smattering of applause.

'C'mon, Yorick,' muttered Willy. 'Now!'

He nervously fingered the bottle of love potion in his tunic. Unless Yorick kicked in soon with the diversion, the chance to reverse the love spell would be lo——

BOOOOOOOOOOOOOM!

The explosion was so loud, it sounded like the world had ended. It was accompanied by a flash of white light that temporarily blinded everyone. Then a great plume of white and pink smoke rose from the forest.

Lord Melonsquidger screamed and dived under Lady Hippolyta Roundbottom's skirts. Egbert Stott jumped in front of the Queen, drew his sword and, half-blinded by the flash, accidentally cut the top off his little finger. Olly fainted dead away, followed by both pageboys. It was pandemonium.

It was Willy's chance.

He staggered forward, fumbling for the stopper on the bottle of love potion. Why hadn't he remembered to shut his eyes? He'd forgotten how bright Yorick's flashes were. As his vision returned, he knew he had no way of controlling which person picked which goblet. Yet again, there was no choice but to splash the potion into as many goblets as possible. His main worry was the Queen. Everyone else could take their chances. As long as the Queen changed her mind about bringing the play forward to the following morning, nothing else mattered. Well, almost nothing.

No sooner had Willy re-corked the bottle and stashed it away, than the smoke began to clear. Yorick stepped out from the trees with an embarrassed grin. 'Sorry to halarm you, me most precious sweetness!' he shouted to the Queen. He waved the smouldering flashpot in the air. 'Jist tryin' out some o' me special-heffects powder!'

'Whoo hoo!' whooped the Queen. 'That was incredible, Mr . . .?'

'Yorick,' said Yorick, beaming. 'Jist Yorick, Ma'am.'

'Well, Mr Yorick,' said the Queen. 'One shall want one of those explosions at one's wedding tomorrow!'

Yorick shuddered, but managed to throw a ghost of a smile in the direction of the Queen. 'As you wish, Yer Majesty,' he croaked. 'Wotever you desire!'

'One thinks a toast is called for,' said the Queen.

Willy picked up a tray and, doing his best to impersonate a pageboy, he sidled up along-side her.

'A toast,' she cried, picking up a goblet. 'To love!' She took hold of Egbert's hand.

'To love!' echoed the courtiers.

The Queen swigged the wine, set down her goblet, blinked twice and shivered as if someone had dropped a snowball down her knickers. Then she looked down at her fingers, which were intertwined with Egbert Stott's. 'And what,' she hissed, 'do you think you are doing?'

Egbert Stott looked like a man who'd woken up in a cage full of hungry wolves.

Meanwhile, Lady Hippolyta was gazing at Sir Victor Vile with the light of love burning brightly in her eye.

Sir Victor drained his goblet, and then glanced up at her as if seeing her for the first time. 'Madam,' he said, 'is there something wrong with you? You have the look of a lunatic!'

'I *am* mad, Victor!' trilled Lady Hippolyta. She grabbed Sir Victor by his tunic and pulled him close. 'Mad with love, you darling lovely man! I can't tell you how happy our marriage is going to make me!'

For a moment Sir Victor—a man who had once captured a rebel Scottish town armed with only a pencil—thought he was going to faint. Only his years of stiff-upper-lip training at St. Swine's, England's poshest school, saved him. 'M-m-m-m-ma-ma-marr-marriage?' he croaked. He turned to Lord Melonsquidger. 'Squidgy, old boy, I could have sworn I've just heard this one-eyed, wooden-toothed woman spout some nonsense about *marrying me*!'

Lord Melonsquidger regarded Sir Victor coldly. As a result of drinking the toast, *he* had fallen madly in love with Lady Hippolyta himself. 'If you are referring to this angel in human form, Vile, then you must be mistaken. She is a flower, a pure cloud, a . . .'

But as he spoke, Lady Hippolyta took her own swig of wine, and wandered off to attach herself lovingly to Olly Thesp's ankle. Olly himself was gazing in adoration at his own reflection in a mirror.

All around the clearing, people were falling in love.

Charlie Ginnell fell in love with an elm tree.

'Isn't she the most beautiful thing you've ever seen in your life?' he cried, tears of love streaming down his face.

Several Codpieces fell in love with each other, causing a number of fights to break out.

Sir Victor slapped his forehead in disgust. 'Has *everyone* gone completely mad?' he yelled. Then he caught sight of Willy holding the tray.

'You!' he snarled. He bounded across to Willy and pressed the tip of his leather-clad finger to Willy's nose. 'I have a feeling that this *nonsense* has something to do with you, you whey-faced whippersnapper! And when I find out what that is, I'll——'

Sir Victor never finished.

A tiny woman, as wide as she was tall, barged past him. 'EG*BERRRTTTTT*!' she yelled in a voice as hard as granite.

It was Mrs Stott. She was there to do what any Englishwoman would do under the same circumstances: drag her good-for-nothing husband back home, and to give a knuckle sandwich to the person trying to steal him.

'Oi!' said Sir Victor, whipping out his sword and striding after Mrs Stott. He snatched up a goblet of wine from a passing pageboy and took a gulp, then grabbed Mrs Stott by the shoulder. She turned to face him, her fists bunched and ready.

What Sir Victor had planned to say was: 'Clear off, you sawn-off little peasant, before I sling you into the Tower'. What he found himself saying was: 'Your eyes are like twin pools of molten chocolate and your hair is like a waving field of sun-washed corn'.

In reply, Mrs Stott kicked Sir Victor in the kneecap and headed off to find her husband.

Egbert Stott, seeing his wife coming his way, took a quick drink to steady his nerves and fell hopelessly in love with her. It was like falling in love with a comfortable but battered old shoe.

Sir Victor hopped up and down on one leg while Mrs Stott whacked a smiling Egbert over the head with her trusty rolling pin. In normal circumstances, anyone who kicked Sir Victor in the kneecap would be hauled into the Tower sharpish. But since the knee-kicker in question was the love of his life (as of two minutes ago) Sir Victor was, for once, at a loss for words.

While all this highly entertaining knee-kicking business was going on, Willy spotted Yorick at the edge of the clearing, barrelling towards the Queen with a goblet in his hand. In a flash, Willy knew what Yorick was going to do. '*NOOOOO!*' he yelled.

'Anuvver toast, Yer Majesty?' said Yorick as he pulled up in front of the Queen in a cloud of dust. 'To England!'

'Er, quite,' said the Queen. She lifted the goblet to her lips and took a regal sip.

'Your Majesty!' yelled Willy.

'Not now, Waggledagger,' snarled Yorick.

'Can't you see that I'm a-wooin'? Naff off!'

'But——' said Willy.

It was as far as he got.

Yorick grabbed Willy's collar and flicked him headfirst into a pile of horse poop. Then he turned back to the Queen.

'I say!' she began, her voice like honey, 'has anyone ever told you your eyes are like twin . . .'

Willy rolled out of the horse poop and wiped his face. His plan had failed again.

Everywhere people were making kissy noises, singing love songs, strumming lutes and setting off on long, meaningful walks. As the summery day began to turn into a velvety evening, love was in the air. Love was all around.

It was horrible.

The thought of going back to Stratford was starting to look really attractive.

'Isn't it wonderful!' trilled the Queen. She

pinched Yorick's bottom. 'One shall be married! Tomorrow! Hurrah for love! Shortly, one will leave for the night. But one will see you all in the morning, when one will decree that *everyone* can marry whomever they wish!'

There was a loud cheer.

Willy sighed. At least things couldn't get any worse.

'Oi, Diggleslider!' hissed a familiar voice. 'Wot's 'appenin' wiv me Girdle? I'll wage that war, you know! I will!'

10

This Be Egg, Faerie Favours

The King of the Faeries stood behind Willy, with his goat, as always, nearby.

Willy spat out a wodge of horse poop and scowled up at O'Brion. He'd had about as much of this as he could take. Every time he tried to fix a problem, he just made it worse. Maybe he should just take the first oxcart back to Stratford after all. Once his father eventually calmed down, Willy could forget he'd ever even heard of the Black Skulls, and settle down to a life of tanning. Sure, it would be smelly and soul-destroyingly awful, but at least there would be no more getting thrown into piles of horse poop, no more worrying about Queens, or actors, or Faerie Kings, or love, or Golden Girdles. And it wasn't like any of his so-called friends cared about him any more anyway. They were all too busy being in love! Perhaps going home would be for the best.

'Do you want to know what I've done about your belt?' Willy snapped at O'Brion. 'Absolutely nothing! Zero! Zilch! There's been no progress of any kind! Your stupid belt is still wrapped around the Queen's stupid bum! And I'm not going to do so much as lift a finger to *unwrap* it, unless you get off your lazy backside and help me.'

The King of the Faeries was not used to being spoken to like this. ''Elp you?' he said. 'Why should I, King of the Faeries and Emperor of the Forest, 'elp you, a common little actor peasant person?'

'Because it's *you* who wants the belt!' said Willy. 'You've got to give me more time. I can't just go blundering in and grab the thing, now can I?'

Willy noticed O'Brion wasn't listening. He was staring across the clearing to where Yorick and the Queen were huddled together, saying their goodbyes for the night, and giggling like a pair of love-struck nincompoops.

'Wot's goin' on?' said O'Brion. 'Wot is my galumphin' big bruvver doin' gettin' all lovey-dovey wiv the Queen?'

'Oh that,' said Willy. 'That's your big brother getting ready to become King of England.'

'Gadzooks!' squeaked O'Brion. 'We can't 'ave two kings in the family! It wouldn't be natural! I wouldn't like it one little bit!' He swung around and grabbed Willy by the arm. 'Right, Dibbledagger, wot 'ave you got in mind?'

'I don't know,' said Willy. 'He's *your* brother! And this whole mess is thanks to that potion of yours. You are King of the Faeries, aren't you? Do some . . . you know . . . magic.'

O'Brion gazed thoughtfully across the clearing. 'Magic, you say,' he muttered, shaking his head. Several small woodland creatures dropped out of his beard and scampered underneath a trestle table. 'There *might* be summink, I s'pose. But I'm not sure we should even try it. It's too risky.'

'We have to try *something*,' said Willy.

O'Brion plunged a grimy hand deep into the folds of his ratty green robes and pulled out a long wooden stick.

'A wand!' gasped Willy. He'd never seen a real wand before.

'No, it's a stick,' said O'Brion. He threw it over his shoulder and reached once more into his robes. This time he pulled out a black cat.

'A witch's familiar!' Willy drew back.

'Tiddles!' said O'Brion. 'I'd been wonderin' where you woz!' He put the cat down and she wandered away.

'Are you sure there's *any* magic in there?'

said Willy as O'Brion once again fiddled with his clothing. This time he pulled out a small wooden box, tightly bound with string. He carefully slipped the knot and opened the lid to reveal, lying on a cushion of finest velvet, the smallest egg Willy had ever seen. O'Brion delicately picked up the tiny blue-and-yellow-speckled oval between his thumb and forefinger and held it close to Willy's face.

'Behold,' breathed O'Brion.

'An egg?' said Willy doubtfully. 'It doesn't *look* magical.' He reached out to touch it.

O'Brion leapt back from Willy's outstretched hand as if it was a red-hot poker. 'Careful, you milk-faced monstrosity!' he hissed. He gently placed the egg back in the box and closed the lid. 'This is dangerous stuff, boy! This is the hegg of Thompson's Tit—the Greater Crested Thompson's Tit, to be completely haccurate.' He lifted a grimy, ring-encrusted finger and pointed into the distance. 'A great beast of a bird wot lives in the farthest and most 'orrible dark reaches of the forest. Few 'ave seen it and lived to tell the tale. This 'ere hegg is very powerful juju!'

O'Brion took Willy's hand and pressed the small wooden box into Willy's palm. 'Use it wisely,' he said. 'And wait until I'm well out of the way.'

Willy looked down at the little box. He couldn't believe it! Here he was, begging O'Brion for help, and what had the idiot given him? A stupid old bird's egg! What good was that! He jammed the egg into a pocket in his undershorts.

'I should have known better than to ask a great steaming moon-howler like you to come up with anything useful!' Willy shouted, glaring at O'Brion. 'But I forgot—you're completely cuckoo! Why don't you and your stupid goat just forget about this stupid belt, and *get lost*? Just go away! I never want to see you again!'

O'Brion took a step back, and eyed Willy coldly. His pink wings quivered threateningly. 'Very well, Wobbledazzler,' he said quietly. 'You've 'ad yer chance. I'll get me Girdle back meself, no fanks to you. This is *war*!'

And with that, the King of the Fairies stalked back into the forest to rally his troops.

'War, shmoor,' Willy muttered to himself. He'd had enough. For now, he had two things he wanted to do. Firstly, he was going to find a nice cold stream and wash off the rest of this awful horse poop. Secondly, he was going to retrace his steps, find his sack of belongings, and then head straight back to Stratford and leave this ridiculous theatre life behind him forever.

It was all too *complicated*.

Twenty minutes later, Willy reached his bag, and bent down to pick it up. But as he did so, an image of Yorick, in his Pan costume, clopping pathetically after the Queen, popped into his mind.

Willy sat down heavily on the nearest tree stump. He couldn't do it. He just couldn't up sticks and leave his friend like that. Yorick might be acting like a huge pain in the bum right now, but it wasn't *his* fault he was under a love spell. He deserved all the help Willy could give him.

Willy picked himself up, and trudged wearily back to the clearing for the third time that day.

The only place Willy could find to sleep that wasn't filled with carpenters, painters, cooks, maids, gardeners or Black Skulls was an old hollow log right at the edge of the clearing. He clambered in, lay down, and sighed.

Perhaps tomorrow would be a better day.

11

The Curse of True Love

The next morning, Willy crawled out of his log and blinked.

The clearing had been transformed overnight. It was now a love grotto. There were heart-shaped lanterns, pink and white ribbons, silken streamers, draped muslin, shimmering fabrics and tiny tinkling bells that tinkled in such a horrible tinkly-twinkly way that Willy wanted to stomp them into smithereens. A wedding cake bigger than a peasant's hut stood on a white table, almost entirely hidden under an avalanche of white roses.

The Queen had already arrived with her

usual band of lords and ladies. Sir Victor was wandering around looking for someone to shout at.

Willy felt completely overwhelmed. It was all very well him coming back again with good intentions to sort this out, but the problem was enormous. What could one eleven-year-old boy do by himself?

Suddenly a grimy hand grabbed Willy by the ankle and hauled him to the ground.

'*Aaaargh!*' he squealed as he was dragged underneath Eric's cart.

It turned out that the grimy hand was attached to O'Brion. He was hiding amongst a jumble of prop boxes and assorted rubbish.

'Won't you just leave me alone for one minute?' said Willy. 'You frightened the life out of me!'

'Never mind that, peasant,' whispered O'Brion. 'I 'ave news.' He was dressed from head to toe in tree bark that had been stitched together into something that looked a bit like a suit of armour. His wings had been replaced by deer antlers. His face was daubed with blue paint and he had put some sort of dye in his mouth that turned his teeth bright red.

'What have you done to your face?' said Willy.

'War paint, chum,' hissed O'Brion. 'Now be quiet. You 'ad yer chance, and now the time for talkin' 'as passed! It's time for me to stop the weddin' and get me Girdle my way! The mighty army of Richmond Forest wants blood! This is war!'

Willy peered past O'Brion's shoulder at the mighty army of Richmond Forest, which was huddled behind him. It consisted of the one-eyed squirrel, three crows, the hairball dog—his fur shaped with mud into little spikes—and the goat.

'Look, Your Majesty,' said Willy desperately.

'I'm sorry for what I said last night about you being cuckoo. I didn't mean it, honest. Why don't you give me one last try? You know, at finding a peaceful end to all this before you go in with ... er ... all squirrels blazing? For Yorick's sake?'

O'Brion scowled. 'Very well, Fiddleflogger,' he said after a long pause. 'Fer Yorick! You 'ave until lunchtime to get me that Girdle or me and the army are goin' in! Got it?'

'I won't let you down,' said Willy. 'I have a ... er ... most excellent plan!'

Willy smiled bravely as O'Brion and his army crawled towards the cover of the trees. But there was no excellent plan. Willy didn't have the foggiest idea how to get hold of the Queen's girdle.

As he stood brushing grass from his knees, three rather ugly bridesmaids arrived at the cart. It took Willy a moment to realise they were Minty, Olly and Elbows.

'What's happening?' Willy asked, staring at Elbows's frilly dress.

'There's a shortage of bridesmaids,' said Elbows. 'Charlie's insisting that we fill in. It's embarrassing!'

Olly swished his skirts around. 'Oh, I don't know,' he said. 'It could be rather fun.'

'What do we do about the performance?' complained Elbows. 'How are we going to be bridesmaids, change costume for the play, *and* find time to get married?'

'I'm exhausted!' wailed Minty. 'We were up all night!' He eyed Willy suspiciously. 'I didn't notice you practising your lines anywhere.'

Willy looked at Minty blankly. It took him a few seconds to remember he was supposed to play the part of the Queen. 'I ... um, forgot,' he said, lamely. 'I've got a lot to think about right now and ...'

'You think *you've* got problems?' said Olly, glancing down at his bridesmaid's costume.

'You wouldn't believe how long it took to make this! I've had no time at all to do my hair.'

'I'm more worried about O'Brion and his wretched belt,' said Minty. 'It doesn't matter who the Queen is in love with, we'll be slung in the Tower as fast as you can say "I do" if she finds out O'Brion thinks we're on his side in his crazy war!'

'It's no use arguing,' said Elbows. 'We've just got to get on with it. We are the Black Skulls, after all!'

'Black Skulls or not,' said Olly, 'we could all do with as much help as the Queen gets.' He pointed across to the tent that the Queen was using as her dressing room. 'She gets a whole team of dressers to help her, and she's only wearing one frock!'

A steady stream of dressmakers, seamstresses, ladies-in-waiting and pageboys had been flowing in and out of the tent carrying fabrics, hairpins and drinks all morning.

Suddenly, Willy got another one of his ideas. A good one. An *excellent* one. One that just might work. He knew exactly how he was going to stop O'Brion's war. The problem of the weddings would have to wait.

'Elbows, Olly, Minty,' he said. 'Can I have a word?'

12

The Cradle of the Queen

Willy checked himself in the mirror.

His face was hidden under a thick coat of white make-up. His lips were painted a bright red. He was wearing a blue travelling dress that looked just like the one the Queen had arrived in that morning. Olly was a wizard with the needle and thread.

I don't look half bad, thought Willy.

'The dress won't last long,' said Olly. 'I only threw it together.'

'Just a bit more white on the forehead,' said Minty, holding Minimac up for a closer look, 'and you'll be set.' He patted Willy's face with a make-up pad. Clouds of powder billowed around them.

'Are you *sure* this is going to work?' said Olly. 'What if it goes horribly wrong?'

'If we don't keep O'Brion happy,' said Willy, 'he's going to fight this war.'

'With a squirrel!' said Minimac.

'Maybe,' said Willy. 'But whatever he does, it could mean the end of the Skulls. You don't want to spend the rest of your lives locked in the Tower, do you?'

Elbows came into the tent carrying something in a sack. 'Here's that item we talked about,' he said. He reached inside, pulled out something and twirled it in the air. It was a narrow golden belt, tied together with white ribbons and studded with gems.

'It looks just like the real one!' said Willy. 'No one will notice the difference!'

'There's no one better at faking than Elbows McNamara!' said Elbows. 'The Prop

Wizard, they call me. The Jewellery Genius. The Fabulous Faker!'

'I never heard anyone call you that,' said Minimac.

'Well, they do, right?' said Elbows, thrusting out his chin.

'How's it looking outside, Minty?' said Willy, butting in before a fight started.

Minty ducked to the entrance of the tent, carrying Minimac, and used his free hand to lift up a section of the curtain. Then he peeked through a gap. 'Time to go,' he said. 'The Queen's just heading for the Archbishop's tent. I reckon you've got about ten minutes. You know what a windbag he is.'

Olly adjusted Willy's dress. 'I hate to admit it,' he said sourly, 'but you do look exactly like Her Majesty.'

Willy glanced into the mirror one last time. Olly had done a first-class job of turning him into the spitting image of the Queen. He lifted up his dress and tied the sack containing the fake girdle around his waist. He smoothed the dress back over the top and headed out.

It took only a few seconds for Willy to cross the clearing and reach the Queen's tent. But it was long enough for him to decide that his excellent plan was actually a dumb plan. He hesitated and almost turned back.

To his surprise, Olly pushed him firmly towards the Queen's tent door. 'Curtain's up, Waggledagger,' Olly, hissed. 'Chest out, head up, we're on!'

There were two Codpieces guarding the door. Willy expected trouble. But, to his amazement, the two Codpieces stepped aside and Willy passed them without a hitch. Olly was close behind.

Inside the tent, two ladies-in-waiting were making some last minute adjustments to the Queen's wedding outfit. They looked up, saw Willy and sprang to their feet.

'Your Majesty!' said one. 'You look ... that is, I mean, we thought you were——'

'Silence!' snapped Willy, in his best Queen-voice. He glanced at Olly. 'This is er, Mistress Sputum, a distant cousin of my nephew's uncle's half-brother. She's suddenly arrived from, er, Wigan.' Willy waved towards a rack of clothes in the centre of the tent. 'One desires one's, um, wedding garments to be ... applied to one's person.'

The ladies-in-waiting goggled at him. Olly nudged him gently in the back.

'Now!' said Willy doing his best to sound bossy. It seemed to work. The two women began to fuss around him.

'Mistress, erm, Sputum,' Willy said to Olly. 'Check on one's royal jewellery, and make sure some common oaf hasn't stolen it.'

Olly bowed and slid across to a wooden jewellery box that was sitting on a table. He lifted the lid, and there, nestled on a cushion of fine red velvet, was the real Golden Girdle.

'It's here!' Olly shouted, before bursting into a fit of fake coughing.

The ladies-in-waiting looked at him.

Olly took a deep breath. 'Your royal jewels are safe and sound, Ma'am,' he squeaked.

The ladies looked away again.

Olly scuttled to the tent opening, looked out, and got a nasty shock.

The Queen was standing no more than ten paces away, talking to Lord Loudtrouser. Luckily, she had her back to the tent.

Olly glanced over his shoulder, his eyes wide. 'She's on her way!' he mouthed to Willy above the heads of the ladies-in-waiting, who had just finished clothing Willy in the Queen's wedding outfit.

'What!' Willy said in his normal voice.

'Your Majesty?' said one of the attendants.

'Erm, the girdle,' said Willy, back to his Queen voice. 'One demands the Golden Girdle to be applied now to um, the royal person.'

The ladies-in-waiting moved quickly. The Queen's temper was well known, even if she was speaking funny. As they took the Golden Girdle from its box, Willy slipped the fake girdle from its hiding place in his underclothes and passed it to Olly.

While the ladies busied themselves lacing up the real girdle around Willy's waist, Olly slipped the fake one into the box. Elbows had done a superb job. The fake looked exactly like the real one. Olly closed the lid silently just as the last lace was fastened around Willy's waist.

There was no time to lose! The Queen would be arriving any second.

Willy crossed his legs and waved the ladies-in-waiting away.

'Royal toilet break, ladies!' he managed to stammer. 'Bit of privacy, if you don't mind.'

He moved towards the curtained-off part of the tent that—he hoped—contained the royal privy. The ladies-in-waiting stood uncertainly alongside Olly at the tent door.

'Shoo!' said Willy. 'And fetch me my ... er ... wedding bouquet while you're at it! Mistress Sputum knows where it is.'

'Come right this way, ladies,' said Olly, ushering the women out of the tent and using his body to shield them from the Queen. He turned and winked at Willy as he left.

Willy was stuck. He couldn't make a break for it and risk bumping into the Queen when he was dressed in her wedding outfit. Not to mention the fact that he was wearing her stolen Golden Girdle. An icy chill ran down his spine at the thought of being caught red-handed with a valuable royal treasure.

I'll just put it back! Willy thought. He grabbed the fake girdle from the wooden box and lifted his skirts. Then he stuffed the fake girdle into his underpants.

He was just about to return the real girdle

when he heard Lord Loudtrouser calling, 'Fare thee well, Your Majesty!'

'She's coming!' muttered Willy. He grabbed his original costume off the floor, and ducked into the privy, with the real girdle still around his waist.

Inside the Queen's privy, bunches of roses hung from the thick canvas walls. A velvet throne, set on a walnut plinth, had been placed above a wide wooden chute that went out through an opening in the tent and down to a pit.

It was a good privy. And—Willy knew as he heard the real Queen entering her tent— it was a privy in which he was trapped.

'Mistress Bloom! Mistress Moreleigh!' called the Queen.

Willy heard the ladies-in-waiting return.

'Your Majesty?' said Mistress Moreleigh in a puzzled voice. Hadn't they just dressed the Queen in her wedding clothes? Now, for some reason, she was back in her travelling dress!

'Where have you been?' said the Queen. 'One needs to be dressed immediately!'

'But you . . .' said Mistress Bloom before realising that sometimes keeping your mouth closed was the safest option.

'Yes?' said the Queen frostily.

'Nothing, Your Majesty,' said both ladies-in-waiting.

'Very good,' said the Queen. 'Now, prepare my robes while I have a royal poop.'

The ladies-in-waiting puzzled over what the Queen had said. Why would the Queen have asked them to dress her once, then take off her dress and ask them to do it all over again?

In the privy, Willy had an even bigger problem. He was trapped, and the Queen—who everyone knew was the most dangerous woman in England—could discover him any second!

Why didn't I just go back to Stratford when I had the chance? Willy thought to himself.

13

Out of This Privy Do Not Desire to Go

Queens, just like everyone else, need to go the toilet. And, just like everyone else, they prefer to go in complete privacy.

So when the Queen walked into the royal privy, the last thing she expected to see was an exact replica of herself, wearing her very own wedding dress.

'Hello, Your Majesty,' said Willy. He bowed as much as the girdle around his waist would allow.

Normal people, faced with an intruder in their privy—never mind one who is wearing their wedding dress—would have screamed, or run away, or fainted. But the Queen was made of sterner stuff. She was, after all, the Queen. So the shock of finding Willy in her privy simply registered as a slight twitch of her upper lip and a single blink.

'One is most surprised,' she said, sounding completely unsurprised. 'One will call for help.' She turned and parted the curtain. 'Mistress Moreleigh,' she said quietly, 'send for Sir Victor. One has an intruder.'

'Yes, Ma'am,' Mistress Moreleigh replied.

The Queen turned back to Willy. 'Now, explain. And quickly. Sir Victor is not a patient man.'

Willy paused. If he didn't come up with a good story in the next few seconds, he knew he was as good as dead. 'Apologies for startling you, Your Majesty,' he said. 'My name is Willy Waggledagger. We've met before. I was, um ... hiding underneath your skirts in Stratford. I'm only in your, er, privy because I was ... um, trying to stop the ... erm, spies from ... stealing your Golden Girdle!'

'Spies?' said the Queen.

'Yes, Madam! Great big nasty Spanish ones,' said Willy, thinking fast. 'I happened to be passing your tent on my way to last-minute rehearsals for our play. Which is why I am dressed as you. It was supposed to be a small surprise. Sort of a wedding present from the Black Skulls.'

The Queen smiled a little. 'How amusing,' she said. 'Continue.'

Willy began speaking faster. Sir Victor couldn't be far away now. 'And a Spanish spy—a big fellow with a horrible droopy Spanish moustache—saw how I looked like Your Majesty, and forced me into your tent!'

'Where you put on one's wedding dress,' said the Queen. She raised a royal eyebrow.

'Well, yes,' gabbled Willy. 'I was forced to, because ... because of the Golden Girdle!

That's right. To smuggle out the Golden Girdle more easily, I was to dress in Your Majesty's wedding clothes. So I did.' Willy blinked at the Queen hopefully. 'Then I . . . er . . . hit him on the head and . . . er . . . he ran away,' he added.

There was a bustling sound from the main part of the Queen's tent. The next second, the curtain of the privy was thrust aside and Sir Victor Vile bounded in, his sword at the ready.

'Where's the varlet? Let me at him!' he snarled. Suddenly he stopped in his tracks, his eyes darting between the Queen and Willy. 'What sorcery is this?' he growled, pointing his sword first at the Queen and then back to Willy. 'Which of you is the true Queen?'

'*I* am, of course, you idiot, Vile,' said the Queen. 'Don't be ridiculous!'

Willy pointed to the Queen. 'That's right, Sir Victor. She is. The Queen, that is. I'm not. I am . . . er, Willy Waggledagger.'

'The Stratford boy!' gasped Sir Victor. He

lunged forward and lifted Willy onto his toes with the tip of his sword. 'Always around, whenever there's skulduggery to be found! This is the second time you've been caught in Her Majesty's private chambers. Give me one good reason why I shouldn't take your head off this *instant*, cur!'

'Because *I* require your sword, Vile,' said the Queen. She had a steely glint in her eye as she stared at Willy.

Willy gulped.

'Of course, Your Majesty,' said Sir Victor. 'I quite understand. You want to punish this varlet *yourself*.' He handed his sword to the Queen, his teeth bared in a wolfish grin.

'Willy Waggledagger,' said the Queen. 'Kneel.'

Willy dropped to his knees in front of the Queen. Sir Victor rubbed his hands together as the Queen hefted the long sword in her hand and brought it down slowly, until the point rested on Willy's left shoulder. It felt heavy. And sharp.

So this was it, thought Willy sadly. His dreams and hopes were gone, all because of Yorick's idiot brother, O'Brion. At least, no one could say that he, Willy Waggledagger, hadn't done his very best to help his friends. He closed his eyes and hoped it wouldn't hurt.

The Queen lifted the sword in the air. Sir Victor chortled.

The Queen brought down the sword and gently touched Willy on the right shoulder. 'Arise, Sir Willy Waggledagger,' she said.

'Eh?' said Sir Victor. 'What!'

Willy looked up. Had he heard correctly? Had he just been *knighted*?

'What are you waiting for? said the Queen. 'On your feet, Sir Willy!'

'Madam, I ... that is ... you *can't* ... did you?' spluttered Sir Victor. 'You *didn't*? He *isn't*——'

'Stop babbling, Vile,' snapped the Queen. 'Sir Willy here has just foiled a Spanish plot! Which is a lot more than you and your blasted Codfish have been doing! All I've seen you do all day is chase around after that wretched Mrs Stott! She's *already married*, you know!'

'*Ob crsh, Yr Mjsty,*' hissed Sir Victor through tightly clenched teeth. He stalked to the farthest corner of the privy, his head the colour of a baked beetroot.

Willy ran his hand around his neck, amazed that his head was still attached to it. A Knight of the Realm! Who would have believed it? Wait until he told everyone!

'Of course, you must tell absolutely no one of this, Sir Willy,' said the Queen. 'It must remain our secret. That way you can stay one step ahead of the spies.'

'Spies?' said Willy. 'Oh, oh yes, the spies.'

'Now, I need my wedding clothes back,' said the Queen. 'And my Golden Girdle.'

Willy handed her the girdle and began to take off the wedding dress, taking good care to keep the fake girdle down the back of his own underpants. He passed the garments to Sir Victor, and dressed quickly in the Queen's blue travelling costume that he'd been wearing to start with.

'And of course,' said the Queen brightly, 'no one must ever know you were ever in here. No one must see you leave this tent. The spies may be watching.'

Willy looked around, puzzled. Aside from the way he'd come in there *was* no other exit. Then he noticed Sir Victor grinning from ear to ear and pointing past Willy towards the royal toilet. With a sickening lurch of his stomach, Willy realised that there was, in fact, one other way out of the privy: through the waste chute at the back.

Willy did what every Englishman would have done in the circumstances. He bowed to

the Queen, scampered up to the seat of the
throne, lifted the lid with one hand and,
holding his nose with the other, dropped down
into the darkness.

14

NoW ThE HuNgry Yorick Roars

O'Brion wasn't as happy as he should have been about getting back what was, as far as he knew, the Golden Girdle.

He dangled the girdle at the end of a long stick. 'It's covered in summink ... *nasty*!' he said.

Willy was busy scrubbing himself off with a rag and a bucket of water.

'And so are you!' continued O'Brion. 'And I ain't even goin' to arsk why!'

'It is *royal* poop,' Willy said brightly, although he knew better than anyone that royal poop was as smelly as ordinary poop.

He was so smelly that even the goat was standing well back. It was only having been raised in a tanner's house that had stopped Willy from throwing up.

As he cleaned himself, Willy started to feel slightly more human.

O'Brion passed the fake girdle to Willy. ''Ere, you can clean this, too,' he said.

Willy dunked it in the bucket and shook it. 'There,' he said handing the cleaned girdle back to O'Brion. 'Good as new.'

O'Brion examined it closely. 'It's a bit bashed up,' he said. 'I woz expectin' it to be in a bit better condition, to be honest.'

'It's been through a lot,' said Willy.

'Well at least it's back wiv its rightful owner,' said O'Brion. He lifted several layers of his tree-bark armour and tried to fasten the girdle around his belly. After a few moments of stretching and straining, he gave up and strapped it around the top of his leg.

'So, no more war?' said Willy.

'I'll 'ave a job talkin' Tinkerbell out of a punch-up,' he said, pointing at the one-eyed squirrel. ''Is blood's up, y'see? But, no, there'll be no war.'

O'Brion took hold of a long stick lying on the floor and raised it above his head. Willy flinched.

'Calm down, boy!' said O'Brion. 'I ain't goin' to 'it you!' He pushed Willy down on one knee and, just as the Queen had done in her privy, the King of the Faeries knighted Willy.

'Arise, Sir Wigglesligger!' said O'Brion.

Willy got to his feet. He wondered if anyone else had ever been knighted twice in one day. 'Er, thanks, er ... Sire,' said Willy.

O'Brion tippy-toed off towards a tangled thicket. 'Good doin' business wiv you, Sir Fibbleshlinger! I'll see you next time yer in the Kingdom!'

And with a final rustle of leaves, the King of

the Faeries and his ragtag army disappeared amongst the trees.

Willy sighed with relief. O'Brion seemed happy enough with the fake girdle. There would be no war, and Willy's friends wouldn't go to the Tower just yet. It looked like Willy could avoid his father's hateful clutches by staying with the Skulls for the time being.

Now all Willy had to do was stop Yorick becoming King of England.

The big question was: how?

Willy headed into the clearing and lay down, exhausted, in the back of Eric's cart. As the proceedings got underway, he saw Charlie roaming around the clearing looking for him. Willy ducked out of sight. He was in no mood right now to discuss the upcoming play. If he was to rescue Yorick, he needed time to think.

And it would be a rescue, Willy was sure of that. Yorick might look like he was happy about getting married to the Queen, but Willy *knew*

Yorick wasn't cut out for palace life. He was a man of the road, a traveller, a wandering theatre-gypsy. Life at the palace for Yorick would be like life for a gorilla in a cage.

Yorick was sitting beside the Queen on one of two large white thrones at the altar. He had finally been persuaded to take off his Pan costume, and was dressed from head to toe in lace and silk, his hair braided and oiled. He looked like a bear wearing make-up. The Queen looked like a huge white meringue in her wedding dress. Behind her stood the ever-horrible Sir Victor Vile, checking, as usual, for any signs of anti-Queen behaviour. And probably, thought Willy, keeping an eye out for England's newest (and most secret) knight of the realm: Sir Willy Waggledagger.

Suddenly Willy's ears pricked up. Lord Melonsquidger and Lord Loudtrouser were sauntering past the cart. They pointed at Yorick and giggled.

'What a buffoon!' said Lord Melonsquidger.

'I know!' whispered Lord Loudtrouser. 'Can you *imagine* how the children would look?'

'She'd be better off marrying that ox,' said Lord Melonsquidger, pointing to Eric.

They raised silk handkerchiefs to their mouths and tittered, before drifting towards the refreshment tents.

Willy watched them go. So this was what would happen if the wedding went ahead. People would say nasty things about Yorick. People would make up rhymes about him. The palace courtiers would plot against him.

But even more importantly, Willy would miss him. He *liked* having the big oaf around. Willy simply refused to stand by and let his friend get married like this.

He jumped down from the cart and drew himself up to his full height. After all he *was* a 'Sir', a nobleman! And noblemen—even small ones—did what was noble, didn't they?

What I have to do, Willy thought, is break the spell that Yorick is under. He leaned against the cart and pondered. After a moment, he caught sight of the pots and pans he'd cleaned the night before. An idea came to him. He grabbed the frying pan and turned towards the camp fire.

Meanwhile, up on the stage, the Archbishop of Canterbury ran a nervous finger around the collar of his vestments.

'Well?' said the Queen. She prodded the Archbishop in the back with her sceptre. 'Is there a problem, Bertram?'

'N-no,' said the Archbishop. He cleared his throat and looked at the list of weddings. 'Dearly beloved,' he began, 'we are gathered here today to witness the, erm, marriage of one Charles Fortescue Ginnell and ... "Elma", who is, Mr Ginnell tells me, an elm tree.'

The Archbishop smiled thinly and turned to the Queen. 'I—I—I'm not really feeling very well, Your Majesty,' he whispered. 'I'm not sure people are allowed to ... er, um ... marry *trees.*'

'Poppycock and balderdash, Bertram,' said the Queen in her most queenly voice. 'It's love, man, love! Now get moving. One has oodles of lovely weddings to get through today!'

The Archbishop turned back to Charlie. 'And where is your bride?' he asked.

Charlie pointed to a large elm tree draped in white ribbons. 'My one true love, Elma,' he beamed. 'Look at her beautiful leaves! Isn't she lovely? So ... green!'

Behind the cart, Willy set the heavy frying pan across the hot stones. He reached for the lard.

'Get moving, Bert,' snapped the Queen.

'In for a penny, in for a pound, I suppose,' muttered the Archbishop. He turned to Charlie. 'I now pronounce you man and tree. You may prune the bride.'

'Whoo hoo!' yelled Charlie. He ran across to Elma and threw his arms around her moss-covered trunk.

'Hurrah!' shouted the Queen.

There was a loud burst of applause.

Back at the cart, unnoticed by the crowd, Willy dropped a dollop of lard into the pan and watched it melt.

The Archbishop married Lord Melonsquidger to Lady Hippolyta (with Olly as bridesmaid), Walden Kemp to a soot-smudged member of the palace catering staff he'd bumped into shortly after a swig of love potion, and Sir Victor to a grim-faced Mrs Stott. (Mrs Stott was even more grim-faced than usual on this particular occasion. But she was playing along, because Sir Victor had made it plain that Mr Stott would spend the rest of his life in the Tower if Mrs Stott didn't go through with the wedding.)

Willy took three rashers of best bacon and

placed them into the spitting fat. The aroma of frying bacon began to waft across the clearing.

No one could resist the smell of a good rasher or two (or three) of bacon. Especially Yorick. Willy was relying on it.

Trumpets blasted, signalling the main event: the marriage of the Queen to Yorick. As the trumpets faded, Elbows—looking both silly and splendid in his bridesmaid's dress—played his fiddle furiously at the side of the altar. Alongside him Olly, also in his bridesmaid's dress, sang his heart out. The palace bells chimed in the distance. The Queen smiled at Yorick and he smiled back at her. Everything was ready.

As the crowd grew silent, Willy chopped some mushrooms and slid them into the pan. They were followed in quick succession by a thick Cumberland sausage, a ripe red tomato and a slab of black pudding.

At the altar, Yorick's nostrils twitched like a

lurcher dog's when scenting a pheasant. Willy could see his great head lift in the air as the magnificent smell of a glorious Full English breakfast was sucked up into his nostrils.

This will definitely do the trick, Willy thought happily.

The exhausted Archbishop adjusted his pointy hat. Like a boxer getting himself up for the last round, he began the service.

Willy waited confidently for Yorick to snap out of his trance and come bounding across the clearing for some breakfast.

Any minute now, he thought.

Suddenly, Yorick shook his head as if to dislodge some water from his ears. He fixed his gaze back on the Queen and smiled.

Willy couldn't believe his eyes. It wasn't working! The awesome power of the fry-up was failing!

'Dearly beloved,' said the Archbishop, 'we are gathered here today to witness the coming together in holy matrimony of our Most Wondrous Queen, Elizabeth——'

He broke off as Yorick once again sniffed the air. 'Bacon . . .' he whispered softly. '*Bacon . . .*'

'Hurry it up, Bertram!' snapped the Queen. She too had smelled the fry-up and, because she was the cleverest woman in England, she guessed how powerful the effect might be on Yorick. She'd waited years to find someone to marry, and now the moment was here, she would finish the job at all costs. Nothing could distract her husband-to-be until she had the ring on her finger. She peered at the crowd and caught Willy's eye. Even from a distance, he could see her sudden scowl.

The Queen turned and barked an order to Sir Victor. 'Stop that boy!' she hissed. 'Waggledagger!'

'My absolute pleasure, Madam,' purred Sir Victor. He pecked Mrs Stott on the cheek, leapt from the altar, drew his sword and barged his way towards Willy. A brace of Codpieces followed close behind.

Willy gulped. Yorick was clearly responding to the delicious cooking smells. He just wasn't responding enough. Then Willy realised. He had forgotten something. The fry-up wasn't complete! Bacon, yes. Sausage, yes. Tomatoes, black pudding, mushrooms, yes, yes, yes! But there was one vital ingredient missing.

An egg!

Willy rummaged in the store box. But there wasn't a single egg to be found. As Sir Victor and the Codpieces drew nearer, Willy remembered he did have an egg. Just one.

O'Brion's egg. The egg of Thompson's Tit.

The Archbishop was by now rattling through the wedding service like an auctioneer at a cattle market. 'Therefore,' he gabbled, 'if any man can show any just cause why this couple may not lawfully be joined together, let him speak now, or forever hold his peace . . .'

'There's no one!' snapped the Queen. 'Now get moving, Bertram!'

'*DoyouYourRoyalHighnessQueenElizabethofthe HouseofTudordaughterofKingHenryCommanderof theFleet——*'

'Yes, yes, Bertram!' yelled the Queen. 'I do!'

Willy fingers fumbled with the wooden box. Scrabbling with the twine, he pulled open the lid and the tiny egg rolled out onto his palm. It was his only chance. If Yorick sniffed the frying egg, he would snap out of the lovesick haze he was in. Wouldn't he?

'*AnddoyouIsambardRobertoHaroldYorick brotherof . . .*' said the Archbishop.

'Get the traitor!' screamed Sir Victor as he closed in on Willy.

Willy lifted the egg to the edge of the frying pan, got ready to crack it . . .

And dropped it.

Time seemed to stand still. The egg toppled downwards, end over end. It hit the side of the frying pan, cracked open and bounced straight into one of Yorick's flashpots, which was standing in its usual place next to the cart.

And then everything went green.

15

Stinky Musk Roses, with Egg

The instant the egg hit the flashpowder, a bright-green cloud exploded outwards and upwards with a force that had to be seen to be believed. The stink was *incredible*.

It was worse than a mouldy Scotsman's sporran coated in rancid badger fat, filled with rotten brussel sprouts, fried in French cheese, and then left to stand in the hot sun for three weeks in a puddle of sweat from a wrestler's armpit.

Willy, who was standing almost directly above the blast, would have suffered badly if he hadn't been raised in a tannery. His father used to soak rotting animal skins in vats of dog poop outside Willy's bedroom door, but compared to the stink of this egg, those vats were like the finest French perfume.

Willy, knocked flat on his back by the blast, felt as though his head would melt. His eyes blurred and his nostrils felt like they'd been scoured with acid. He got unsteadily to his feet and looked around.

At first, he thought everything had disappeared: stage, singers, trees, Codpieces, cakes, lords, ladies, and even Richmond Forest itself. The world was nothing but a fog of green smoke and total silence. Then, as the fog started to clear, so did Willy's brain.

There had been a wedding, he was pretty sure of that.

Yorick. The Queen. A wedding. No, *lots* of weddings! Then, through the mist, Willy started to see lurching shapes. They were people, slowly getting to their feet.

One thing was for sure: the weddings were definitely over. All the sparkling wedding dresses, all those spiffy tunics and lanterns, ribbons, wedding cakes, musicians, painters and courtiers, were coated in stinky green powder. Men and women wandered uncertainly around the clearing, groaning and checking themselves for damage.

'Oh dear, Waggledagger,' hissed Charlie Ginnell, as he stumbled into view. 'What did you *do*? The Queen's going to go completely doolally raving bonkers mental!'

Willy's heart sank. He agreed. Doolally raving bonkers mental was the least of his fears. He looked around for the Queen, and spotted Olly Thesp comforting himself in a mirror. The rest of the Skulls were coming to their senses and discovering that the person (or tree) they had married didn't look quite so lovely as they had a few moments ago. Sir Victor and the Codpieces were still out cold on the ground. Willy hoped they wouldn't remember much when they came around.

But there was no sign of the Queen or Yorick. Perhaps, Willy thought with a sudden panic, they'd both melted somehow in the explosion. Maybe the Queen was extra sensitive to smells. He'd heard she was a very clean-living woman. Although that wouldn't explain Yorick's disappearance.

Then suddenly a patch of green fog lifted and there they were. The Queen was sitting in a puddle of spoiled wedding dress. She blinked at Yorick, whose braided hair had come loose, and whose fancy wedding silks were crumpled and ruined.

Willy wondered if it was maybe time to slip away and take his chances at home with his father. He was fairly sure that setting off an exploding egg at a Queen's wedding was, at the very least, a hanging offence. He shivered at the thought of what punishment might await him.

Time to skedaddle, he muttered to himself.

He turned to make a dash into the forest ... and bumped straight into Sir Victor.

'Going somewhere, *Sir*?' croaked Sir Victor. He leaned forward and peered at Willy. 'Not before we've had a little word with Her Majesty. I can't recall exactly *how* you're involved in this disaster, you pewling little pipsqueak, but I will find out!'

He dragged Willy towards the stage.

'Is Your Majesty injured?' said Sir Victor, drawing his sword a few inches out of its scabbard with one hand, and lifting Willy clean off his feet with the other. 'Has this raisin-visaged little slime-weed *attacked* your royal personage?'

The Queen struggled to her feet and wiped her face.

'Waggledagger,' said Yorick, as he lurched upright. 'Woz that your little idea?'

'*Are* you responsible for this?' asked the

Queen. She waved her hand around at the ruined decorations and coughing courtiers.

This is it! thought Willy. The end of the road. I'm a total failure and I should have stayed in boring, safe old Stratford, where I belonged! So much for saving my friends from the Tower of London and staying with the Skulls. Now I'm going to die horribly, and my friends will probably still get sent to the Tower for the rest of their lives, just for knowing me.

Sir Victor shook Willy. 'Answer, peasant!' he hissed.

'Er, yes, I'm afraid it was me, Your Majesty,' Willy muttered.

'See?' said Sir Victor. 'Told you.'

'I'd just like to point out that this was entirely the boy's idea, Your Majesty,' said Charlie, who had been watching events unfold from the other side of the clearing. He trotted across and poked his head over Sir Victor's shoulder 'Nothing whatsoever to do with the Black Skulls! Nothing!'

'Thank you, little commoner!' said the Queen to Willy. 'You have saved one from making the biggest mistake of one's whole entire life!'

'Amen,' said Yorick, ripping a crumpled ruff from around his neck.

'Can one imagine,' continued the Queen, 'the embarrassment of being married to ... *that*? The commonest commoner one has ever seen! One would never be able to face the Spanish Armada again! You have saved one!'

'Yeah, well,' muttered Yorick, moving across to stand next to Charlie. 'Yer not the only one who's been saved, Missus!'

'Wait a minute,' said Sir Victor, lifting Willy up again and shaking him. 'This runt must be punished for ... *something*!'

'Nonsense, Vile,' said the Queen. 'He's done precisely what you should have been doing.

Aren't you here to protect me, *hmm*? Now put him down and keep quiet.'

Sir Victor turned purple and released his grip on Willy. 'Of course, Your Majesty,' he said through gritted teeth.

'Now what about your bride?' continued the Queen. 'What on earth will Mrs Stott, er ... I mean ... Lady Vile think of all this?'

Sir Victor Vile staggered as if he'd been struck by a musket ball. He looked around the clearing frantically. Mrs Stott, her rolling pin mislaid in the blast, was some thirty paces off to one side, energetically beating Egbert Stott on the head with the blunt end of a ham hock she had found lying nearby. Egbert seemed to be happy with the thrashing. It meant that things were getting back to normal.

'M-M-Mrs S-*Stott*?' Sir Victor managed to croak. 'My *bride*? That was a dream, I thought! She—I—we ... that is, we didn't, did we?'

'Oh, yes, Vile,' said the Queen, nodding.

'Quite the little married lovebirds you were.'

Sir Victor's hand flew to his mouth. He ran to the nearest bush and vomited loudly.

Charlie stepped forward and put his arm around Willy. 'Always rely on a Black Skull, Your Majesty! We'll never let you down!'

'Wot's all this "we" business?' muttered Yorick in Charlie's ear.

Charlie's smile never wavered. 'Show business, Yorick, just show business,' he whispered. 'Just smile and keep Her Nibs happy and we might come out of this with some ching in our pockets for once!'

The Archbishop of Canterbury was slowly getting to his feet. He picked up his pointy hat, which now had a large dent in it, and put it on his head. The Queen kicked him in the ankle.

'*Ow!*' he yowled, hopping up and down. 'What was that for, you—you—I mean . . . Your Most Gracious Majesty?'

'You *idiot*, Bertram!' said the Queen. 'What

were you thinking of, marrying one to this *yeti*?'

'I am still 'ere, you know!' said Yorick. 'I do 'ave feelins!'

'Oh, be quiet,' said the Queen. 'If you don't pipe down this instant, one can arrange for your head to be on a spike in the Tower by this afternoon.'

Yorick kept quiet.

'You're the Archbishop of Canterbury!' the Queen continued. 'Didn't you let someone marry a tree? It's your job to make sure things like that *don't* happen!'

'Yes, Your Majesty. I don't know quite what came over me,' muttered the Archbishop. 'Of course, all the marriages are now dissolved.'

'Good,' said the Queen. 'One will be keeping an eye on you in future, you naughty little Archbishop.' She crooked a finger at Willy. 'One needs a word with you, young man. In private.' The Queen led Willy behind a large oak tree at the edge of the clearing.

'What do you think she's up to now?' said Charlie. 'I hope he's not in more trouble!'

A few moments later, the Queen and Willy emerged from their conference.

'Now,' said the Queen, briskly. 'Has anyone seen one's horse? One wishes to get back to the palace. One is quite exhausted by all this wedding nonsense! Never again!'

The Queen and her flock of dishevelled lords and ladies headed off.

Willy bowed.

As Sir Victor passed Willy, his moustache quivered furiously. 'This isn't over, peasant,' he whispered. 'Your day will come!'

But Willy didn't care. O'Brion's egg and Yorick's favourite flashpowder had done their work. No one was in love with anyone. The pong had wiped all thoughts of sonnets, poems, lovey-dovey songs, lutes, and wedding cakes clean out of everyone's mind.

He was about to dance a jig of victory when there was a dull thud. Yorick had slumped face-down in a pile of green-spotted musk roses.

Willy dashed to his side and shook him furiously. 'Wake up, Yorick! Wake up!'

'Waggledagger,' croaked Yorick weakly. 'The hegg . . .

'What about the egg?' cried Willy.

Yorick sniffed the air, and sat up. 'Any chance of rustlin' up annuver Full English?' he said. ''Cos if there is, I'll 'ave a plateful. Wiv extra fried bread. I'm famished!'

all shall Be well

Eric the ox was once again going as fast he could. This time he was leading the trundling procession of Black Skulls carts towards London.

Which was just fine with Willy. Eric could go as slowly as he liked, in any direction he liked, just so long as they were travelling away from Richmond Forest.

The Skulls were heading to London for their next big gig: a week-long stay at London's swankiest new theatre, the Billericay Bowl. Willy couldn't have been happier. Apart from the itchy feeling he had in his bum.

He shifted his position on the driving board.

'Will you keep still?' said Yorick. 'It's like sittin' next to a bloomin' June bug on a skillet!'

As usual, Yorick was sitting at the front of Eric's cart alongside Willy. The rest of the carts were strung out in a line behind them. All traces of the love potion had vanished, and the farther they travelled, the more dreamlike the last couple of days seemed to become. Had they *really* met the King of the Faeries? Had Charlie Ginnell really married a *tree*?

'You know summink, Waggledagger?' said Yorick. 'You did me a favour back there. Take it from me, one king in the family is more than enough.'

Yorick looked over his shoulder. O'Brion stood at the edge of the forest, watching as the Skulls came to the top of a rise in the track. O'Brion locked eyes with Willy, and gave him a military-style salute. The fake girdle was still wrapped around the top of his right thigh, gleaming in the woodland light. Then, as the carts rolled down the hill towards the river, O'Brion and the forest disappeared from view.

'*And* I didn't have to go back to Stratford,' said Willy.

'Not yet, anyway,' said Charlie popping up from where he sat behind them in the back of the cart.

'Moanin' again, Charlie?' said Yorick. 'One of these days yer goin' to surprise us all and be satisfied wiv summink.'

'What have I got to be satisfied with?' said Charlie. 'Another Black Skulls gig and no money! Her Majesty didn't pay us, you know. *"No play, Mr Ginnell,"* she says. *"You didn't perform your play."* Blooming toffs. All thanks to Waggledagger here! He might as well be a blooming toff too, for all the use he is!'

'Sir Willy Waggledagger ...' murmured Willy. 'Sounds good to me.'

'What?' said Charlie.

'Doesn't matter,' said Willy, smiling to himself.

'We *did* get the Billericay Bowl,' said Yorick.

'Only because I twisted Lord Melonsquidger's arm,' Charlie said. 'He's part-owner of the Bowl and he thought the weddings were the funniest thing he's ever seen. But we still came away from Richmond Forest without so much as a brass bean! Where's the money going to come from to keep this show on the road, that's what I want to know? We might not *make* it as far as London. I suppose you think I can pull money from my backside?'

Willy shifted his position for the twentieth time in as many minutes. 'Funny you should say that, Charlie,' he said.

'I suppose you're going to produce money from *your* backside, are you, Waggledagger?' Charlie scoffed.

'In a way,' said Willy. He handed the reins

to Yorick, stood up and braced himself against the rolling motion of the cart.

'Gentlemen,' he said, dropping his pantaloons and pointing his rear end at his audience.

'Sweet screamin' sticklebacks,' said Yorick. 'You crafty little ankle-biter!'

Charlie didn't say anything. He was too busy staring at Willy's bum. The Golden Girdle was wrapped around it, sparkling in the sunshine.

'Is it . . .?' stammered Charlie.

Willy nodded. 'Remember I got Elbows to make a copy of the girdle? My plan was to swap it for the real one. But when I got into the Queen's tent, I chickened out and gave the Queen the real one back. I gave the fake to O'Brion instead. He seemed happy enough.'

'So 'ow on earf did you get this?' said Yorick.

'You didn't steal it again, did you?' asked Charlie anxiously.

'No,' said Willy. 'The Queen *gave* it to me

just after the explosion. It's kind of a reward for saving her from a fate worse than death: marrying Yorick.'

'You cheeky divot!' said Yorick. 'So that's wot you woz doin' wiv the Queen behind that oak tree! I wondered wot you woz up to!'

Charlie couldn't speak. He didn't often get emotional, but this was more than he could stand. He grabbed Willy and crushed him to his chest. 'You *lovely* little Black Skull!' he wailed. 'You're a genius, my boy! You were born for the theatre!'

Yorick chuckled and gave the reins a snap. 'You might want to pull up those pantaloons, genius,' he said. 'We're coming closer to London and yer brains are flappin' in the breeze.'

about the author

Martin Chatterton has traced his family tree back to the days of William Shakespeare and, in an amazing coincidence, has found that the greatest English playwright was not his great-great-great-great-great-great uncle! Born in Liverpool, only a stone's throw from Stratford (assuming the stone was launched via a grenade launcher), Martin has been doing joined-up funny writing for absolutely yonks. Martin loves Shakespeare because, if the Bard was ever stuck for a word, the cheeky monkey would just invent one! Martin's favourite Shakespearean word is 'road'.

about the artist

Gregory Rogers was born in Brisbane, Australia, which is nowhere near Stratford. His favourite Shakespeare play is *A Midsummer Night's Dream* because it's got such great characters. Like Shakespeare, Gregory loves inventing good characters and in over 20 years of illustrating books he's created lots. One of his books even won the prestigious Kate Greenaway Medal in England. He bets Shakespeare never got one of those!

Look out for ...

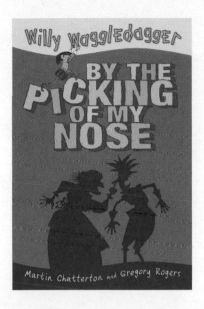

Willy Waggledagger has accidentally tickled the Queen's bum with his false beard.

Now Willy is WEARiNg a frock,
Sir Victor Vile wants to chop off his head,
a doll is plotting to betray him,
and an old witch wants to pick his NOSE.

Could this be the true story behind Shakespeare's *Macbeth*?

available NOW!

Coming soon ...

Willy Waggledagger

Chew Bee or Not Chew Bee?

Willy Waggledagger has finally made it to the big smoke.

Now Willy has SEEN a ghost,
everyone thinks he has gone mad,
a dog is in love with Yorick,
and Willy ends up with a mouth full of bees.

Could this be the true story behind Shakespeare's *Hamlet*?

Praise for
Willy Waggledagger —
By the Picking of My Nose

'This zany novel is bursting with slightly revolting humour and mayhem. A fun introduction to the world's greatest ever playwright.'

—*Bookseller & Publisher*

'This is an awesome book. Sometimes it made me laugh and other times it made me laugh even more.'

—*Jacob Harris, age 9*

'I give this story five stars!'

—*Edward Warrington, age 11*